Temptation

By Leda Swann

Don't miss the next book by your favorite author.
Sign up now for AuthorTracker by visiting
www.AuthorTracker.com.

LEDA SWANN

Temptation

AVON

An Imprint of HarperCollinsPublishers

HarperCollins books may be purchased for educational, business, or sales promotional use. For information, please write: Special Markets Department, HarperCollins Publishers, 10 East 53rd Street, New York, NY 10022.

FIRST AVON PAPERBACK EDITION PUBLISHED 2009.

Designed by Diahann Sturge

Library of Congress Cataloging-in-Publication Data
Swann, Leda.
    Temptation / Leda Swann. — 1st ed.
        p. cm.
    ISBN 978-0-06-167240-8
    I. Title.
    PS3619.I548T46 2009
    813'.6—dc22

                                                2009012884

09 10 11 12 13   OV/RRD   10 9 8 7 6 5 4 3 2 1

One

The faint yellow gaslight caught the grains of white sand falling into her lap as Beatrice Clemens opened the envelope. Sand from half a world away. Carefully she collected the grains, placing them on the bedside table where they gleamed against the dark mahogany wood.

She treasured getting letters from her far-flung siblings, particularly from Teddy, doing his duty for Queen and Country in far off South Africa. Teddy described it as a harsh land, so hot and dry over the summer months that it was practically a desert. The ever-present sand worked its way into every item of clothing, adding its mite of discomfort to the irritation already caused by too much heat and insufficient water.

Her roommate, Lenora, looked over from where she was slumped in her armchair by the window. She had propped her feet up on a footstool and was wriggling her swollen ankles. The brightly patterned curtains were pulled, shutting out the night and enclosing them in the pallid yellow mist of artificial lamplight. "Is that really sand?"

"Yes, sand. All the way from the Transvaal in southern Africa." How strange it was that her only brother, the baby of the family, and her favorite sister should both wind up in Africa. And how different their two lives were. Louisa lived in a world of love and beauty with her land-owning Moroccan husband, while Teddy endured a harsh life in the army at the other end of Africa, keeping an eye on the rebellious Boers.

Carefully unfolding his letter, she kept an eye out for more sand. The grains in her letter had most likely fallen out of his hair when he rumpled it as he wrote. The thought of it brought a wistful smile to her face. As a small boy, Teddy had always rumpled his hair whenever he was concentrating hard on something.

"What is his news?" Lenora had leaned over and was massaging her ankles. Her red hair was creeping out of her bun in messy tendrils and her uniform was a mess of wrinkles, and stained down the front from a spill.

Beatrice scanned the letter quickly. "They have been sent off into the interior, into some tiny settlement, where there's nothing to do but look threatening while the Boers talk openly of rebellion. The camp sounds terribly dull. He writes that he misses the society they enjoyed in Pretoria."

Lenora looked up from her feet. "I'd rather be a nurse than a soldier any day. Despite the sore ankles." She gestured at their room, which, though small, was nicely furnished with knotted rugs on the floor, handsome mahogany furniture, and lace covers on the backs of the chairs. "Even though our days are long, at the end of them we can come back to home comforts, rather than being stuck in a camp out in the desert. And I *like* tending to the sick. They are always grateful that someone cares about them."

The two of them had come off the end of a long shift on the wards at St. Thomas's hospital—dressing wounds, spooning medicine into patients' mouths, and tending to their personal hygiene. There was never enough time to sit down for more than a few minutes together, and Beatrice's ankles were aching, too. Still, being a nurse was satisfying work and, like Lenora, she wouldn't swap it for any other career. She'd wanted to be a nurse for as long as she could remember. "I must write back to him. He sounds like he needs a letter from home."

She drew a chair up to the little writing desk and pulled out a sheet of paper. Though she loved her work, it wasn't really anything to write about. She tickled the tip of her nose with the end of her pen and hummed a music hall ditty to herself to brighten her spirits.

Her work was just the same routine, day after day. She did what she could, but there was always more sickness and death to contend with. All she could do was alleviate the suffering of those for whom she cared, and help cure those who could be cured.

Lenora pulled the hairpins out of her hair one by one, and shook her dark red hair down over her shoulders. Thick and lustrous, it shone in the yellow gaslight like a river of fire. "You could tell him about nasty old Mr. Tomlinson turning purple in the face and dropping dead of an apoplexy right before our eyes. That gave me quite a start, I can tell you."

Beatrice choked back a scandalized laugh. Neither of them had liked Mr. Tomlinson. He had always shouted at them rudely and pinched their bottoms when they made up his bed. "It's hardly a fit subject for a letter. And I'm sure Teddy doesn't want to be reminded about death. He must think about it quite often enough as it is. I know I would in his position."

"You could tell him about the new doctor who just joined the staff." Lenora's voice was sly.

"Dr. Hyde?" Beatrice wrinkled her nose. The new doctor was quite handsome in a serious kind of way. More importantly, he was clearly hardworking and ambitious—just the steady, settled sort of man she had decided long ago that she would marry. She had been quite excited when just yesterday morning he had asked her to go walking in the park with him on Sunday.

But that wasn't something she could write to her baby brother about. She hadn't even told Lenora, and Lenora was not only her roommate but also her best friend. An invitation to go walking was hardly newsworthy, and it would probably come to nothing.

Lenora gave a dreamy sigh at the sound of his name. "Marlene told me he comes from a good family in the Midlands, and that his father is a very successful attorney. He could've bought a church living or a commission in the army or anything, but he chose to become a doctor. He wanted to spend his life healing the sick." She sounded as though she was half in love with him already.

Ruthlessly Beatrice tuned out the sound of Lenora's rhapsodies and turned to her letter. What she really wanted was to have her sister Louisa home again. It was a joy to have her visit every summer from her home in Morocco, but that seemed an age ago. Still, now that spring was upon them she would soon return, after a particularly lonesome and dreary autumn and winter. She had looked after Louisa for so long—it had been her sister's weak lungs that had made her decide to become a nurse in the first place. Though she had scores of patients passing though her ward every week, without Louisa to care for, her life seemed somehow lacking.

An hour later, she put aside her pen, her letter to Teddy finished. Lenora had already clambered into bed and was snoring gently over her book.

With a sigh, Beatrice extinguished the lamp, flung off the shawl she had wrapped around her shoulders, and wandered downstairs to the communal parlor. A good fire and the pleasant company of the other lodgers in the house were what she wanted now. That, and a hot cup of cocoa to help her sleep.

Percival Carterton meandered through the hot streets of the small South African town with one of his acquaintance in his regiment, idly kicking the dirt with his boots. A dust cloud puffed up into the air with each step he took, drifting away slowly on an eddy of the still air, and then gradually fell back to the ground again. It was hot, and some of the dust rose high enough to stick to the thin sheen of sweat on his face and neck.

He pulled uncomfortably at the neck of his regimental jacket. The dark red fabric absorbed the heat of the sun, making him swelter in the summer heat. The white cork hat of his uniform at least kept the sun off his face, but it made his head itch.

They passed a couple of cherry-cheeked girls standing at the doorway to a modest house and Carterton smiled at them through force of habit. They were not pretty girls—their faces were broad and flat, their hair an indeterminate shade of brown under shapeless bonnets, and their figures well hidden under lumpish gowns of a drab gray color—but still they were female and thus worth a smile. Back home in England, where pretty girls were two a penny, he would not have given them a second glance, but here in the Transvaal he could not be so choosy.

The pair of them did not appreciate his courtesy. One of them muttered something dourly under her breath, a Boer curse, he had no doubt, and then spat after him into the roadway.

Charming manners the local girls had. Just charming.

He sighed and kicked the dust harder as he walked along. Life in the high veld of South Africa was interminably dull and dreary. The local Boers, descendants of the original Dutch settlers, hated them, resenting the law and order that the English and their soldiers were bringing to the land.

Even at the best of times the Boers were a sober bunch of people, more likely to pray than to party, and more concerned with sin than with socializing. They did not know how to let their hair down and enjoy themselves. Fun was a foreign concept. Everything about them was drab and gray: their faces, their lives, even the landscape that surrounded them. And they had no more manners or conversation than a stye full of pigs.

His companion, Edward Clemens, a young lad of barely eighteen, punched him lightly on the arm. "Don't sigh after them. They're only a couple of draggle-tails not worth bothering with. Any one of my sisters would be worth twenty of such sour-faced drabs."

"Yes, but your sisters are not here, are they? Anyway, it's not them. It's this damn country," Carterton replied moodily. "It's too damn hot. It's too damn dusty. And the girls, even the ugly ones, treat us like lepers. It's enough to drive a man mad."

"It's not England, that's for sure," Clemens agreed. "It's too sunny, for starters. Can you remember a day in England when it didn't rain?"

"I wouldn't mind a bit of honest English rain right about now to dampen down the dust." He kicked a cloud of it into the air just to see the dust motes glitter in the sunshine. "If only we could get out of this godforsaken town and do something. Anything."

They had passed through the dusty town to the outskirts. A bare, flat land stretched out in front of them, the odd small hillock the only feature to break the monotony. From here, the mildly undulating landscape looked as flat as a table top.

"If only we could get posted down south and fight the Zulus just to see a bit of action. Or be sent off to Afghanistan or India, or even to New Zealand to fight the Maoris. At least there would be the chance for a bit of glory. But to be forced to wait for weeks on end in the middle of nowhere, garrisoning a town that does not want to be garrisoned . . ." Carterton's voice trailed off in despair.

"And all the girls looking as if they'd squashed their faces flat with their mother's iron," Clemens added for good measure.

In spite of his gloomy mood, Carterton felt the faint beginnings of a laugh twitch inside him. That was one of the things he liked most about young Clemens—the boy could laugh at anything. With renewed energy, he chose a likely looking piece of flat ground and paced off the length of a cricket pitch. He may have found himself in the wilds of South Africa, and wearing regimental colors of dark blue trimmed with scarlet rather than whites, but damn it, he could still play cricket.

At each end he pierced the dry earth with a stake to loosen it before driving the wickets deep into the ground, and balancing the bails carefully on top of them. God forbid that he should damage the wickets by smacking them into the sun-baked ground without loosening the hard soil first. Ronald Rimmer, the dolt, had cracked one of the wickets just last Sunday, and the rest of the regiment had damn near brained him for his carelessness. He'd been sent to Coventry for a week, with no one, not even the ancient laundress who did their weekly wash, speaking so much as a single word to him.

Clemens took the oiled cloths off the treasured regimental cricket bat made of the finest willow, and gave it a few practice swings. Other regiments might treasure their colors above all else, but in this regiment their cricket bat was their god.

He picked up the cricket ball, its red surface cracked and chipped with use, tossed it up in the air and caught it again, as the rest of the regiment slowly congregated at the spot he had marked out.

A few non-regimental spectators had gathered as well, to watch the one amusement that this town could provide. None of the dour-faced girls, Carterton noticed glumly, were among them. A couple of young lads watched the proceedings eagerly, swinging sticks at the ground as if they were practicing to bat.

A small dog yapped and ran over the pitch, raising one hind leg threateningly on the wickets. He lobbed a clod of dirt to chase it off before the wickets could be profaned.

The captain of the other team approached him in the middle of the wicket. "Winner bats first," he called, as he tossed a coin high into the air.

"Tails," Carterton called, as the coin spun in a glittering arc.

Tails it was. He strode up to the crease, bat in hand.

The bowler ran down the pitch and let the ball fly toward him.

He stepped forward, swung the bat, and connected with a loud thwack. The ball sped off across the veld, neatly slicing between a pair of fielders and bouncing away across the lumpy ground.

He started to sprint toward the other wicket, but was stopped by the umpire's shout. "A four."

He strolled back to the crease, smiling with grim satisfaction. Some of his anger at the dour-faced girls had dissipated at the force of the blow. There had been nothing special about those two girls to have them put him in such a temper—it was just that he was starving for female company and companionship.

While they had been stationed in England, there had been any number of pretty girls ready and willing to flirt with an unattached young officer in his regimentals. And if he had wanted something more, well, some of them had been equally ready to part with their favors for a few pretty words and the price of a pair of silk stockings.

Here on the veld there wasn't a single pretty girl to flirt with, and no hope of buying even the plainest trull to warm his bed at night. He could not claim to be especially promiscuous, but he'd never gone so long before without a fuck. His balls ached just thinking about having a lusty young woman under him again, feeling her breasts in his hands and thrusting into her warm, welcoming pussy until he came with a rush.

Dammit, he'd give a week's pay just to talk to a pretty young woman, and to have her smile at him in return. What wouldn't he give to fuck one?

But in the meantime, there was a game of cricket to win. He swung the bat again, sending this next ball spinning high into the air. A fielder dived for it but missed, and it smacked harmlessly into the ground.

Dusk was falling before the cricketers called it a day, packed away their wickets, oiled their bats, and rewrapped them in their protective cloths for the following Sunday. "Good game," he said to Clemens, as they strode back again to the barracks, his temper restored by the severe thrashing they had handed out to the other team.

The lad grinned at him, wiping the sweat out of his eyes with the back of his hand. "I wasn't out for a duck, so that makes it a good game in my books."

"There'll be a tot of rum on me tonight in the mess," Carterton said. "Pass the word to the others while I go and sweet talk the keeper of the stores. Eight o'clock sharp, mind, or you'll get nothing but water."

Clemens shifted uneasily from one foot to the other. "I ought to dash off a quick letter to one of my sisters first," he said uncomfortably, "but I guess it can wait until next Sunday."

Carterton sighed, the gloom of the morning starting to descend on him again at the reminder of his celibate state. "You're damn lucky to have a sister who writes to you. I'll save you a tot of rum and you go write to your sister."

Two

Dear Beatrice,

You're a real brick to write to me. I always look forward to your letters. Some of the others here don't have sisters to write to them and they miss home dreadfully. The captain of the regiment let me off my duties this evening to write to you because he doesn't have any family to speak of. Percy Carterton he is—a capital fellow. You might want to send him a letter, too, if you're in a writing mood. If I'm lucky it might get me off another evening's duties!

Nothing happening here. Still no action. The weather stays hellish hot and there are no girls to keep a man's mind off the dust and the flies.

Your loving brother,
Teddy

Beatrice refolded the letter and tucked it back into the pocket of her skirt. How she loved to hear Teddy's news of his doings in faraway South Africa, even if he spoke of nothing but the mundane details of his existence there. To her, who had never traveled out of England, even his complaints of the heat and flies were imbued with an exotic allure. It was all so unlike the gray and the rain of London.

She would love to see the world as he was doing, to visit countries she had only ever dreamed of. But as a nurse, her work was here in London. She never regretted her chosen profession, but sometimes, just sometimes, she wished she had the freedom—and the money—to travel. How exciting it would be to get on board a steamship with her carpetbag in hand, and know that when she got off again, she would be in another land.

Of course, that was just dreaming. She could never be brave enough to toss away the security of a job she enjoyed to go gallivanting around the world.

Her short break over, she attacked her ward duties once again. One of the old men in the ward had soiled his bed linen, sending the acrid stench of stale urine wafting through the entire ward. She beckoned Lenora over to help her. Together they undressed and washed him, stripped his bed, and tucked a clean sheet around him with military efficiency.

Dr. Hyde was standing in the corner of the ward ostensibly examining the patient in the next bed over, but she could feel his eyes wandering over to where she and Lenora were bending over the bed. She and Lenora worked most of their shifts together, and Dr. Hyde seemed to find endless excuses to be in their vicinity. Though every word he spoke to them was professional, he could not stop his glance from darting in their direction more often than was strictly necessary.

Lenora smoothed her hand over the bedclothes. "He's staring at you again," she murmured. She could not keep a hint of envy from her voice.

Beatrice smiled a secret little smile, turning away from her friend so her satisfaction didn't show too clearly. Although Lenora tried valiantly to hide it, she had not grown out of her obsession with the doctor. Listening to Lenora talk, you would think he was a saint. According to Lenora, every remark he made was somehow portentous, every action of his imbued with selfless concern for others.

Beatrice wasn't as starry-eyed as her friend was—it wasn't in her nature to be starry-eyed about men. She was a pragmatist, a realist, without a romantic bone in her body. She wasn't even sure she believed in love. It was all very well for other people, but it was not for her. Still, as far as she was concerned, everything was turning out very well indeed.

Dr. Hyde had turned out to be a most satisfactory addition to the staff at St. Thomas's hospital. Not only was he a dedicated and capable doctor with the knack of making his patients open their hearts to him, but he was also good company.

Though he was shorter and darker than Beatrice preferred her men to be, and his humor occasionally verged on the dry and sarcastic, he was the best marital prospect of any of the men she knew. He was young, single, and possessed all his own teeth. And, best of all, he had clearly taken a shine to her. If nothing else, she had to admire his taste.

Love or no love, marriage to a respectable man had to be every woman's goal. She could not be a nurse forever, had no parents to leave her any money, and no desire to be dependent on her more fortunate sisters or brother in her old age. Somehow she had to provide sensibly for her future while she was still young. Marriage to a man like Dr. Hyde would be a very good thing—for both of them.

His first invitation to go walking in the park with him had turned into a second invitation, and then a third. They were now generally accepted to be walking out together. It was a measure of Lenora's affectionate nature that she had never reproached Beatrice for snaffling the man she adored. Lenora seemed content to adore him from afar.

Beatrice glanced at Dr. Hyde out of the corner of her eye. Strangely, his gaze seemed to be focused on Lenora rather than on her. It must be a trick of the light, she decided. Even though it was painfully obvious to everyone in the hospital that Lenora was carrying a torch for Dr. Hyde, he had never noticed her in return. Unless avoiding being alone with her counted as negative notice.

They finished making the bed and both of them stopped to watch him for a moment. He was examining a patient with a large tumor in his abdomen, a tumor that was clearly eating away at whatever life the poor man had left. Carefully he palpated it, then murmured some soothing words into the patient's ear.

Despite his obvious pain, the patient gave a genuine smile as Dr. Hyde spoke.

Dr. Hyde looked up at the pair of them. "Would you please assist me for a moment, nurse?"

Before Beatrice had taken in what he wanted, Lenora was there beside him. "Yes, doctor?" Her face bore a look of utter adoration as she gazed up at him, but he did not notice. He simply gave her a few instructions in a measured tone, and she nodded her head and hurried to do his bidding.

Beatrice left the pair of them together by the patient's bedside, and walked moodily down the corridor to the storeroom to fetch another chamber pot for the elderly patient whose linen they had just changed. Odds were on he wouldn't be able to get out of bed in time to use it, but it helped his dignity to know that it was there.

Dr. Hyde was a good doctor, there was no denying it. He had the rare ability of putting patients at their ease, whatever anguish they were suffering. He even dealt well with Lenora's obvious partiality, treating her with a respectful distance.

Annoyingly, though, Beatrice wasn't the least bit in love with him—not as Lenora so painfully was. It would make her world immeasurably brighter if she could convince herself that she loved him. She liked him, she respected him, but that was all. She didn't long to see him when they were apart, or dream about him when she was in bed at night. She wasn't dying to feel the press of his lips against hers, or to enjoy the hardness of his body against hers.

It wasn't that she found him repulsive in any way—she was merely indifferent to the idea of having him touch her. It might be pleasant enough in its own way, she supposed, but that was the strongest feeling she could summon about him.

The penny dreadful novels that she and Lenora devoured in the evenings waxed lyrical on the feelings that a woman should have for the man she was about to marry, but Beatrice didn't believe a word of it. Pretending such feelings existed and were strong enough to make women throw caution to the wind sold more books, she suspected, but they were no more real than unicorns or fairies.

She squelched the little sigh of disappointment she couldn't help but feel. For some reason she couldn't quite fathom, Teddy's latest letter had unsettled her.

She wasn't a romantic, she knew that, but why couldn't she fall in love with Dr. Hyde? Be dizzy in love, head over heels, full of passionate adoration? Even just fall in love with him a little bit? Her older sisters had all found men they adored. Louisa was mad for her Moroccan Bey, and Emily was just as crazy about her Yankee photographer. They had both braved the disapproval of society to be with their chosen partners.

Beatrice wasn't nearly that brave. Fond of him as she was, she wouldn't flout any conventions to be in Dr. Hyde's company. Part of his attraction was how acceptable it would be to be his wife, for she would certainly have him on no other terms. She would never become his lover without the benefit of clergy. The idea would horrify him as much as, if not more than, it did her.

Dr. Hyde was eminently respectable, and as his wife, she, too, would be above reproach. Their union would establish her once and for all firmly as a member of the professional stratum of society. The doctor would not gamble away their money, or drink it, or lose it on unwise investments—like her, he was far too full of good sense for that.

The doctor would never lose all his money and then shoot himself in the head leaving his children to starve, as her own father had done. She would be able to rely on him. He would take care of her.

A good solid brown, like rich earth—that was the color the doctor reminded her of. No flashy scarlet or bright blue, but worthy, dependable brown. Such a practical, useful color. Perfectly suited to her practical, unromantic nature.

She supposed she would get used to the idea that, as her husband, he would have free access to her body. Even if she didn't find much pleasure in it, she was prepared to do her duty without complaint. It was little enough to trade for a lifetime of security.

It was all so predictable, though. She scuffed the toes of her shoes against the rough floor. Was it wrong to want more excitement in her life? To travel to far-off lands? To be more than a nurse in a London hospital? To meet a man for whom she would be willing to throw away all her dreams?

She would write to Teddy's friend she decided as she walked purposefully back into the ward, whistling under her breath, and slid a clean chamber pot under the patient's bed. In her letters, a small part of her soul was free to go traveling the world and visit all the exotic places she could only dream about, while the rest of her remained grounded in respectability.

Then she could do the sensible thing and encourage Dr. Hyde's affection for her, with the view to one day becoming his wife. She liked him quite well, she respected his intelligence and his ethics, and he would not beat her or treat her badly. She would be safe with him. Marrying him would be the most mature response to her situation.

Some dreams deserved to remain out of reach.

Percy Carterton sat in his tent, rereading for at least the hundredth time the letter he had received that morning. Though the sun had gone down and the evening gloom was descending so he could barely pick out the words, still he stared at the paper. Not that he needed the light to read by—he already knew each word by heart.

Dear Captain Carterton,

I hope you don't think I am too forward for writing to you, but my brother Teddy mentioned you might appreciate a letter from home, if only to remind you how cold and gray the early English spring can really be.

It has been raining for a fortnight now, and I would give anything for a dose of sunlight. But there are blossoms on the trees and the clean rain is washing away the soot from a thousand chimneys. Oh, I do love the springtime! Teddy says that it is sunny all the time where you are—almost too hot to play cricket. It sounds quite delightful. I wish I could see it with my own eyes instead of merely hearing it through his descriptions . . .

With all his heart, Percy wished that she was here with him, too. He would delight in showing her the veld, and seeing it anew through her eyes. She would see the beauty even in this harsh landscape, and he would love it for her sake.

. . . But I must close now. It is getting late, and I must be off early in the morning to St Thomas's hospital, where I am working as a nurse. It is not a glamorous position, but I feel that in my own way I am helping to ease the world's burden of suffering.

Did she realize how much this short letter of hers had eased his heart of its burden of loneliness? Just to know that back in England, a beautiful young woman spared him the odd kind thought?

Beautiful she certainly was—he had seen the evidence for himself. After receiving the letter in the morning, he had quizzed Edward about his sisters until the lad had finally reached into his jacket pocket and drawn out the photograph of them all, which he carried close to his chest. The five young women looking out at him from the photograph had all been fine-looking, but he had known at once which one was Beatrice even before Teddy had pointed her out. There had been something in her eyes that had shone through even in the black-and-white image—a fierce compassion coupled with such tenderness that it brought tears to his eyes.

He knew at once that Beatrice was the woman of his dreams, the woman who would make his life complete. The feeling of her reaching out to him through the picture was so strong that he had to fight the urge to snatch the photograph away from Edward and tuck it into his own jacket pocket, next to his heart.

Something of his thoughts must have shown in his face, for the lad gave him an odd look as he put away the photograph. "I told you they're a bit of a contrast to the dour-faced Boer women in these parts."

"They certainly are." None of the women he had seen in South Africa could come close to matching them. "Not a scowl among them."

"Of course it is fairly old now. My sisters had it taken for me before I shipped out here. To remind me of my family back home."

"Your sisters are very beautiful. Particularly Beatrice," he could not help adding.

"You think so?" Edward tilted his head to one side in thought. "Dorothea has always been considered the beauty of the family, though she is such a hellion the man who took her on would have to be a brave soul."

Percy disregarded Edward's opinion. What did the lad know? He was only their brother. Dorothea was well enough in her way, but his Beatrice had the beauty of a saint.

Temptation

Do not feel obliged to write back to me if you do not wish to. I know you soldiers must lead very busy lives compared to us left at home and I do not expect you to become a slave to the pen in your leisure hours.

Kind regards,
Miss Beatrice Clemens

Percy looked away from the letter for a moment, his eyes filling with tears. Beatrice had written him a letter—simply because she thought he might want to hear news of home. It was more than any of his cousins had done, and they were young ladies of leisure with nothing more important than picnics and dances to while away their hours. Even his elder brother only ever wrote him the briefest of notes when he had some important information about the estate to impart.

Of course, he had not been on good terms with his elder brother for some years—it was a wonder Albert wrote to him at all. But the root of their quarrel was in the past. There was no point in picking at old sores and reopening old wounds. Beatrice, beautiful Beatrice, was his future.

He lay back on his narrow cot, the image of her face still strong in his mind. Her hair had been loose in the photograph, falling over her shoulders in a silky sheen. How he would love to run his hands through her unbound hair, his fingers tangling in its soft waves.

His imagination didn't stop at touching her hair. He wanted to touch all of her. In his mind's eye, he could see her standing before him, a naughty glint in her eye, and her hands at her throat slowly undoing the bodice of her dress. She was teasing him, tantalizing him with her nearness, egging him on to making love to her.

With a quick glance around him to make sure he was alone, he unbuttoned his trousers and took his cock in his hand. It was already engorged, and a few strokes made it hard and needy.

He felt a brief pang of guilt at his actions, as if he were betraying a friendship. Young Teddy wouldn't like to think of him fantasizing over his sister Beatrice in such a manner, but the lad would never know, and what he didn't know couldn't hurt him. Every soldier in the field deserved to take his pleasure where he could find it.

His eyes closed, shutting out the view of his tent and transporting him back to England in the springtime, in a glade in the woods on his brother's estate. The sunshine was dappled through the trees, and he was there with Beatrice, the two of them, alone together. There was no sound but the rustling of the leaves and the occasional chirp of birdsong.

He imagined Beatrice slipping the bodice from her shoulders and stepping out of her skirts, leaving them pooled on the grass at her feet. Her drawers would be tucked and frilled and trimmed with lace, and her chemise would be cut low enough to show her breasts—a far cry from the plain nurse's uniform she presented to the outside world. Her elaborate underwear showed the secret part of her that she showed only to him. Enticing. Irresistible.

He would touch her then. Her pink-tipped breasts would fill his hands. He would bend down to lick her nipples into tight peaks, and then he would pull her body against his hard cock, thrusting it against her stomach. She would be soft where he was hard, giving where he was taking.

Then, oh joy, he would slip his hands between her legs, through the slit in the top of her drawers, and stroke the soft mound covered in fine hair. She would be wet, and as he stroked her, she would clutch on to his shoulders and make little mewling cries of need.

Then she would ask him to take her. No, she would beg him to take her. She would get on to her hands and knees with her legs spread apart, and with one hand she would spread open her nether lips in invitation. Her cunt would be glistening with wetness and she would cry out that she wanted him inside her, that she needed him inside her.

He would discard his trousers with frantic haste. His cock would be huge and hard as he thrust into her from behind. She would scream as he penetrated as deeply as he could go, bucking with her hips to drive him in even harder. She would want him so badly she would be weeping with desire, just as he would be.

He was stroking himself frenetically now, as he imagined thrusting into her, pushing into her virgin cunt with his huge, engorged cock. She would love being fucked, and would urge him on with frantic cries. Then her soft pussy would clutch at his cock, convulsing around him, milking him of his juices.

His breath caught in his throat and time stopped for a moment, before it all came flooding back with a rush of orgasm. At the last moment he rolled to one side so the sticky stream buried itself in his blankets rather than shooting up into the air and splattering all over his dress uniform.

Once the tremors had stopped racking his body and his breathing had returned to normal, he gave a sigh and reached for a handkerchief to clean himself. He wanted to spill himself in Beatrice's delicious wet cunt, not in his own damn hand.

He wadded up the handkerchief and threw it into the corner of the tent, then tucked his now limp cock away into his trousers again. While he was stuck out here in the wilds of South Africa without her, he would have to tame his passions by himself.

The sooner this damned war was over, the better. Then he could return to England and court Beatrice in person. In the meantime, he would dream about her when he was alone, and court her through his letters.

With just a few words written to a stranger, she had reminded him of everything that was good about England, everything that he had joined the army to serve and protect. He hoped his own letters would touch her heart in the same way as hers had touched his.

Truly, his Beatrice was a sweetheart. He did not know what he had done to deserve such kindness, but he would not quibble with his good fortune. With a simple letter out of the blue, she had won his heart. Absolutely and irrevocably.

He struck a match and lit a lantern, then took up his pen. He would answer her right away, and let her know how much she meant to him. He might have lost his heart to her, but he would win hers in return. He would make her as in love with him as he was with her.

She was an angel.

She was *his* angel.

Three

Bronkhorstspruit, Transvaal, April 1880
Dear Miss Clemens:

What a wonderful surprise to receive your letter of March, and so grand to read of the spring at home. I can smell the clean refreshing air from here! I did not find your letter too forward, as I already feel I know you remarkably well from Teddy incessantly talking about his sisters back home.

You should know that Teddy is a fine batsman, and a true gentleman when finally he is caught out—even on the rare occasions when he's out for a duck. Unbelievingly our cricket is played on the dustiest of wickets under a harsh dry sun. Not a blade of green grass is to be had, and the flies are most bothersome!

Aside from the monotonous food (our cook has little idea of how to prepare a meal beyond boiling a mound of potatoes in a large pot), the heat beating down on us in our red woolen jackets, and the boredom of marching to and fro with no enemy to engage, our life here is not too bad. The worst we have to complain of is the dullness and lack of society. We are all looking forward to the end of our tour of duty and returning to the green shores of England, and most of all to our family and friends.

How wonderful it is that you are a nurse at the esteemed St. Thomas's. You must have a heart of gold to care for the sick and injured. I know of several soldiers who have had their wounds treated at your hospital, and to a man they have the highest regard for the nurses who treat them so well. With love, even.

Your letter touched my heart. Please, write to me again. Until I hear from you once more, every minute will seem like an hour.

Yours in eternal gratitude,
Percival Carterton

P.S. If I were to be so unlucky as to one day be injured, then I should want to have you to tend to my wounds, as I imagine you are as kind and softly spoken as you are beautiful. If you have the inclination, I would be honored if you would include a photograph of yourself in your next letter, so that I may kiss your sweet lips a thousand times a day. I would keep it close to my heart as a remedy against bullets. An image of your beautiful face would surely protect me against a hoard of Boers and their rifles, be they ever such fine marksmen.

Beatrice sat in the communal parlor of her lodging house, letter in hand, surrounded by a gaggle of the other nurses who boarded there. Even the matron of the lodging house, Mrs. Bettina, who could be quite severe and stern when she thought her charges were being too flighty, sat forward in her chair, listening to her read.

"'. . . your letter touched my heart. Please, write to me again.

'Yours in eternal gratitude,

'Percival Carterton'"

As she drew to a close, one of the girls sighed happily. "He sounds so dreamy. I would love to have a soldier for a sweetheart."

"He is not my sweetheart," Beatrice protested, with some alarm. "I have never met him. I only wrote to him because Teddy said he never got any letters from home and seemed rather blue. You know I am walking out with Dr. Hyde."

Maybe it had been a mistake to read the letter out to her fellow lodgers, even though she had judiciously expurgated it as she went. She didn't want anyone to get the wrong impression, or to read more into their exchange of letters than it merited. She was merely consoling a lonely soldier with a few idle words, and pretending that her letters could make a difference.

"You have all the luck," Lenora said, her voice tinged with envy. "I wish Dr. Hyde had chosen me to go out walking with." She reached for another piece of shortbread and took a contemplative munch. "But with hair the color of mine, and a bottom the size of an omnibus, it's no wonder he chose you instead."

"You have a perfectly normal-sized bottom," Beatrice protested, elbowing her friend in the ribs. Though Lenora had generous curves, she had a small waist—a perfect hourglass figure. The lumpish uniform they had to wear at the hospital hid the finer points of her figure, but then it hid everyone else's, too.

Lenora pulled a face. "Yes, for an omnibus," she muttered through a mouthful of shortbread. "Dr. Hyde clearly thinks so."

"Hang Dr. Hyde—he's a dry stick," said another. "I wish I could write to your soldier, too, and get such a letter back. There's nothing quite like a redcoat to make a girl happy."

Even the matron looked a little misty-eyed. "Our poor young men. They are sent over to foreign countries to protect us and our way of life, and expected to live there without any of the comforts of civilization. How they must miss their friends and family back home."

By now Beatrice had tucked the letter safely away in her pocket. "Teddy says that some of them don't have any family at all. Or none that care enough about them to send them letters or to knit them new socks when their old ones wear out and the army has none to give them."

"It's a crying shame, the way they are treated."

"They shouldn't send our boys to war if they can't look after them properly."

"Then we should be their family," the matron said firmly. "We should write to them and let them know they have not been forgotten, even though they are far from home. If the army has no socks for them, we shall knit them. I am sure they will be grateful for the attention."

The girls all perked up at this suggestion and a mutter of approbation ran through the group.

Temptation

The red-haired Lenora gave a rare smile that lit up her face as if a gaslight had been turned on behind her eyes. The radiance made her look almost pretty. "My uncle is a hosier. He will give us wool at a good price if we explain it is for the soldiers. He fought in the Crimean War when he was younger."

Her suggestion had the ideas flowing thick and fast.

"I have heard that their rations are poor. Maybe if we asked people for donations we could send them some tinned food as well as knitted socks."

"We can do a collection around the hospital."

"One of my relations imports tea and coffee. We could ask him to give us some coffee."

"But how will we know where to send our letters and parcels?" one of them cried.

Beatrice smiled at their enthusiasm. Who would have thought her sudden impulse to write a letter to a lonely soldier would have led to all this? "I will ask Teddy, and he will tell me."

Later that evening, Beatrice sat in her bedroom and smoothed the letter out on her lap. She had not been entirely open with her friends. Captain Carterton had written a postscript that she had not shared with them—it had been altogether too personal to read out in company.

Reading his words again caused a tingling in her limbs that she didn't altogether like. She was sure it wasn't the sort of feeling that a well-bred woman ought to have.

Dr. Hyde would never say anything so personal to her—more's the pity. Though she had gone out walking with him for some weeks now, he had always been scrupulously polite and had never so much as kissed her glove. He *was* a bit of a dry old stick, she supposed, but he was at least a gentleman and he treated her with great courtesy. He had no bad habits that she knew of, but was spoken of by everyone as a respectable person.

Besides, she had to admire a man who made it his life's work to heal the sick and discover the nature of disease. He was not only respectable—he was a good man.

Captain Carterton, for all that he was Teddy's friend and captain, did not seem like such an estimable man as Dr. Hyde indubitably was. What kind of a man would write such words to a woman he had never met? They were almost the words that a lover would write to his sweetheart.

Men like the captain were two a penny—they would court a girl passionately for a few weeks, and then throw her over without so much as a by-your-leave. They were fly-by-nights, will-o'-the-wisps, as insubstantial as dandelion seeds.

As a nurse, she'd seen firsthand the damage that such passionate courtship could do to a foolish young woman. She was too canny to be caught in such a trap—no husband and a baby on the way.

Still, she could not resist reading through the postscript again, and the tingling intensified. Teddy would surely not be happy if he knew what his captain had written to her. Mrs. Bettina would be terribly shocked. And as for Dr. Hyde? He would doubtless think twice about his invitations to walk out with him were he to know of it. Dr. Hyde was a respectable man, and the man she was planning to build a future with.

It was folly even to think of writing back to the captain and giving him any encouragement.

Of course, no one but Captain Carterton himself need ever know. If she were to write to him and ask him to keep her letters private, he would surely heed her request. He was an officer and a gentleman—not some common riffraff of an enlisted man pulled out of the gutters of Manchester or York to be enrolled as a simple foot soldier.

Besides, he was far away in South Africa, and with the Boers on the brink of declaring war, his regiment would not be posted back to England any time soon. What harm was there in keeping a lonely soldier happy, and giving him something to look forward to on the long, cold nights on the high veld?

A thrill of the forbidden ran through her.

He could be her secret fantasy, her foray into tabooed territory. She could write back to him as warmly as she dared—as naughtily as her mind could devise—and Dr. Hyde need never find out.

With that comforting thought, she unscrewed the top from her bottle of ink, and began to write.

She hesitated for a long moment after she had signed her name to the bottom of the page. Then, quickly, before she could change her mind, she scrawled a postscript.

There, it was done. If he did not reply to her letter, she would refuse to be disappointed. That would show he was only a man made of flesh and blood, and not worthy of her dreams.

But she hoped her fantasy man was up to the challenge.

★ ★ ★

Sergeant-Major Tofts rolled out of his army cot, his every joint creaking in protest. Though he had spent his life in the army, he was starting to wonder if he was getting too old for it now. His poor bones weren't the same as they used to be. Even just getting himself up in the morning was getting more difficult. Sometimes he felt that he would trade in his whole kit for a week's sleep on a soft feather bed.

But if he were to leave the army, what then? He had no family, no home to go to. He knew nothing else, had learned no other trade to keep him from starvation. No, it would be his fate to wear his uniform on his back until the day he died, leaving a small sum in the four percents to his second cousin. Few would even notice his passing, and fewer still would mourn.

It was a depressing thought for such a fine morning. He gave himself a mental shake as he fetched a bowl of cold water and shaved the stubble from his cheeks. He had a job to do, and the lives of his men might well depend on how well he did it. The army had no time for malingerers. He wouldn't tolerate it in his men, and he wouldn't tolerate it in himself.

A few minutes later he was sitting at the mess table with his men, shoveling food into his mouth. A shipment from England had just arrived and the men who had received letters or parcels from home were in high spirits. Their jocularity infected the whole table, and though he grumbled at them to keep the noise down, everyone knew they were good-natured grumbles and no one took any notice of him.

Temptation

He was sipping the last of his coffee when Private Willis wandered over to him and tossed him a small packet. "Letter for you, Sir," he said, as he wandered off again.

Sergeant-Major Tofts almost dropped it in his surprise. Who would be writing to him? He looked at the address on the envelope, but it was not one he recognized. Carefully, as though it might blow up in his face if he mishandled it, he opened the envelope. Experience had taught him that good news didn't generally come in unsolicited messages.

The paper wasn't edged with black. That was a relief—it wasn't a note to inform him that any of his friends or relatives had died. But the handwriting wasn't familiar and when he scanned the signature, he didn't recognize that, either. With a growing sense of curiosity, he began to read.

My dear Sergeant-Major,

You are no doubt surprised to receive this letter and little parcel out of the blue, but there is a small group of ladies here in England who would like our boys abroad to know they are not forgotten.

One of our number knows another in your regiment, who provided us with the names of men in his company so that we might write to them. I chose you to correspond with as we are in similar positions, although I would not presume to consider mine is as fraught as yours.

My name is Mrs. Bettina, and I am the matron of a boarding-house near Westminster, London. Like you I consider myself to be responsible for the welfare of my charges, as well as the running of disciplined operations. My poor husband, George, passed away from consumption quite some number of years ago, leaving me to run our boardinghouse alone.

Although there is no one to share my cold bed at night I am lucky to have my ladies to keep me company, and so I am not lonely. There is always a multitude to do, from keeping the accounts to purchasing food from the markets. From dawn to dusk my life is busy and full, it is only in the quiet of the night that I find myself alone.

George used to love to wear the warm woolen socks that I became an expert at knitting. I found I have not lost the skill over the years, and so it was my pleasure to once more take up my needles and make for you the enclosed small token of my regard for our men such as yourself who serve Queen and Country across the reaches of the Empire. I do so hope you find them to your size and liking.

I'm afraid I know little of your conditions there, my imagination is full of exotic birds, large carnivores, and giant spiders. If there is one thing I abhor, it is spiders. I know from books there can be sand as far as the eye can see, and I profess I find that hard to imagine. A sea of sand! What that must be like!

My dear George used to shoot at ducks and quail with a shotgun and hated getting sand in the moving parts, so I daren't think what it must be like for you living in a sandy environment and trying to keep your rifle clean.

I fear I have prattled on far too much. It would be wonderful if you could spare some time and write a few lines in reply.

Yours,
Mrs. N. Bettina

When he had finished, he folded the letter again and put it in his pocket. So, the women of England thought about the soldiers abroad, did they, and cared for their comfort and well-being? It came as a surprise that he cared so much to know.

He'd like to meet the woman who had written to him so kindly. Her letter had struck a chord in his soul.

He'd never been much of a man for book learning, but he could read and write tolerably well. Well enough not to disgrace himself anyway.

He rose from the mess table with barely a grimace of pain at his still-stiff joints. Come this evening he would borrow a pen and paper from one of the officers and write her a reply.

Captain Carterton pushed aside his breakfast of deviled kidneys and snatched the letter from the silver tray with indecent haste. Leaving his unappetizing meal to congeal in its fatty gravy, he slit open the letter with his breakfast knife.

"Business calls," he barked at his fellow officers as he left the mess hall and made his way back to his tent to read Beatrice's words in peace.

Westminster, London, May 1880
Dear Percy,

How wonderful to receive your reply. I was in the middle of my shift when my landlady arrived at the hospital with the welcome news there was a letter from South Africa waiting for me at home. It was torture to have to wait until I had finished my duties, where-

upon I ran home as quickly as I was able and immediately retired to the privacy of my room to open the envelope and savor the words you had written. I sat on the edge of my bed and carefully unfolded your pages. I can but scarcely imagine the conditions under which you put pen to paper, and yet your penmanship is impeccable!

I laughed at your description of Teddy and his batting ability, I am sure you are exaggerating his abilities. My memories of us children playing cricket are that he would always be out on the first or second ball and then leave the game in a terrible huff. He found it severely demoralizing to be beaten by his elder sisters, even though we were twice his size.

I do so hope you are never injured in battle, please do not even think such things. I have seen the beautiful bodies of young men scarred and disfigured by bullet and bayonet, and these are relatively simple wounds suffered during accidents in training exercises. I shudder to think of what happens to an untreated wound without proper care and attention.

The poor wretches I have helped to heal are laid out under the ether, their naked bodies exposed while the surgeons repair their injuries. I do so hope that I never see your body in this state.

Please do not think of me as an improper woman, talking of such matters, but I am a nurse, trained to heal. The male body is one of God's most beautiful creations, and it is so sad to see it broken.

Thinking of you,
Beatrice

P.S.—I blush to the very roots of my hair to write this, but I suspect it would be rather nice to see your soldier's body, as long as it was not on the operating table. B.

The postscript brought a smile to his heart. She was bold, his Beatrice. Bold, and just a little bit saucy. She was no shrinking violet, but a woman with a frank appreciation of the good things in life and the wisdom to let a man know what she wanted. As a nurse she would be used to seeing male bodies, old or sick though her patients might be. There was no false modesty about her, no pretences.

He liked a woman who enjoyed lovemaking as openly as he did. Beatrice, he could tell by her tone, would be such a woman.

He lingered over the letter as long as he dared before he strode on to the parade ground, his hair slicked back, his moustaches waxed, his uniform freshly laundered and free of wrinkles, and his boots gleaming with fresh polish. The precious letter was tucked for safekeeping into his jacket pocket.

His men were sprawled on the scanty grass, their uniforms in the dust. He frowned at their slackness and called an order at them to come to attention, his voice ringing through the veld.

One by one, they lazily got to their feet and slouched to attention. One of them didn't even bother to get up from his seat on the ground, but gave a halfhearted attempt at a salute from where he sat.

Standing back, he surveyed them with a critical eye. Months of boredom and inactivity had softened them and made them unfit for anything.

Their uniforms were messy, and their boots dull and coated in dust. Even their rifles, on which their life would one day depend, bore the telltale signs of neglect. All in all, they looked like a bunch of draggle-tailed misfits rather than a crack regiment of British troops.

As their commanding officer, their shabbiness and lack of discipline was his fault. He had let them get into this state of moribund boredom, verging on despair. Indeed, he'd fallen into it himself for some time, before Beatrice's letters had awakened him to a new sense of purpose, a new sense of belonging.

Starting from today, it was all going to change. Whatever the merits of the conflict in the Transvaal—and of late he had begun to wonder just how justified England's position was—he was going to live to return to England.

Beatrice kicked off her shoes and stockings and lowered her feet into a basin of steaming water. Though it was midsummer, the weather was cool enough to make a warm footbath a lovely treat. Lenora was working nights again, leaving her with a few evenings to herself.

She reached into her pocket and drew out the letter that had arrived in the late post. Their lodgings had turned into a hive of activity for the Royal Mail: letters were received there almost every day for one or other of them. An envelope with a foreign postmark was no longer a curiosity to be wondered over by the whole house, but could be enjoyed by the recipient in secret.

Temptation

Bronkhorstspruit, Transvaal, June 1880
Dearest Beatrice,

How wonderful to receive your letter, just to think of summer back home warms my spirits. We've moved into winter here, and the nights are bitingly cold under our thin blankets. Even with all my clothes on, I lie on my stretcher and shiver all night with only your letters to keep me warm.

Especially your postscript, so forward you were. But not too forward, be assured I do not think less of you. I confess I did blush a bit when I first read it, although after some thought I imagine seeing your womanly form would definitely be rather nice. I like such directness in circumstances such as mine, and I hope that you do as well.

But I shan't complain of the cold too much, for despite the conditions under which we live there is still plenty of wonder in the world to raise a man's spirits. One of the most striking sights to behold in this dusty country is the night sky. When there is no moon the sky is the blackest of black from horizon to horizon, but there are so many stars blazing with a steady light. In some places they are so closely packed that they are like talc carelessly spilt over a mahogany sideboard. What it would be to have you at my side. We could stay close, warming each other while we talk of inconsequential things and let the world carry on without us.

You write in your letter the male body is one of God's most beautiful creations. Naturally I would differ, and venture to say the female form, with its soft curves and enticing scents, is surely the epitome of creation.

And with that thought in my head I shall try to sleep. I sincerely hope you have the time and inclination to reply, and if you do, please be bold! Cast aside social graces and write the things you want to write. I promise to do the same if you are agreeable.

All my heart,

Percy

Folding up the letter again, she tossed it onto her desk. He certainly had a silver tongue, did this soldier of hers. His letters gave her a window into another life, into his thoughts.

She wiggled her toes in the warm water and hummed a popular romantic ballad under her breath. There was hardly a romantic bone in her body, but something about the captain's missives made her think quite longingly of love and romance.

The heat of the afternoon sun was at its peak when Captain Carterton and his men returned to the parade ground after their midday meal. The white cork hat kept the worst of the sun off the captain's face, but he could still feel the harsh rays burning his fair skin. Even though a year in South Africa had tanned his face a few shades of brown darker than normal, the fierce sun still had the power to burn his skin to a crisp.

He had his men set up targets at the far end of the parade ground and then lined them up to fire.

One by one, the men stepped up to the plate, aimed in the general direction of the target, and pulled the trigger. Time and time again, the shot went wide and the target remained unscathed.

"This is target practice," he admonished them, as yet another man stepped up, took desultory aim, and fired. "The point of the exercise is to aim at a target. To aim at and to hit the goddamned target. Not to fire in the air and hope to wing a passing undertaker bird."

It was hopeless. The men were too used to firing in a volley and relying on the density of the enemy numbers rather than on their skill with the rifle to make a hit. Half of them didn't even know how to sight their rifles.

He picked out the best marksman and had him demonstrate to the other men how to aim and fire with some degree of accuracy.

The demonstration made little difference to the number of holes punched in the target.

"We don't have unlimited supplies of ammunition. Make every bullet count," he advised the men.

Neither did his advice help much.

The sun was beating down on the back of his neck until he felt as if he were broiling on a grill. All he wanted was a bit of shade in the cool of the tent, and a long, cold drink. Preferably one with a good tot of gin in it. And a generous dash of bitters.

In desperation he tried a different approach. "None of you will be dismissed for the day until each and every one of you has managed to hit the target at least once."

This threat had the desired effect. Now even the worst shots among the men took several seconds to properly sight their rifles and take careful aim at the target. Slowly but surely, the line of men who had hit the target at least once grew longer, and the line of those who had yet to make the hit grew shorter.

His uniform was hot and prickly on his skin, and soaked with sweat. He shrugged his shoulders uncomfortably, suddenly desperate to escape the discomfort. Why on earth could they not be issued summer-weight uniforms to wear in the heat? Cotton would be so much more comfortable than wool.

The men in the regiment were calling out advice and encouragement to the ever-dwindling line of poor marksmen. Some of them fired off twenty or thirty shots, still without marking the target.

He groaned at this evidence of his men's unpreparedness for war. Again, he only had himself to blame. He should have driven them harder, despite the heat and the boredom of their posting. The rumors that war was imminent were getting stronger by the day. They had to be ready for when the fighting started.

His sweat was chilling on his body by the time the last man hit the target. The men all let out a cheer, and he joined in heartily.

With his objective achieved, and just in the nick of time, he had the corporals quickly assemble the men into a column in preparation to marching them off the shooting range and over to the parade ground. It was nearly sunset and the various units of the company from the kitchen hands to the infantrymen were forming up in straight lines on the parade ground, their red tunics forming blocks of geometric color over the dusty ground.

Raising and lowering the Union Jack was an important ceremony—it was the only time when the company assembled all together. Percy's chest swelled with pride each time he saw the massed ranks of the company, the power they represented stretched from the dirt on which they stood all the way back to England.

The company came to attention, the soldiers presented arms while the officers saluted and the Union Jack slowly made its way down the flagpole as the lone bugler played the mournful "Last Post," signaling the end of yet another day. Satisfied all was well, the company commander dismissed the parade. The assembled men turned a smart ninety degrees to the right and marched the obligatory three paces before dissolving into an untidy mob.

Percy called his men closer. "Clean your rifles well. There will be an inspection of your kit tomorrow morning, and then more target practice until you can all hit the target from double the distance. With every shot."

With the rumors of a conflict growing, shaking the men out of the round of desultory inspections, halfhearted parades, and mind-numbing patrols was essential.

Having had little to do in recent times, they'd all gotten lazy. Each day their standards had slipped just a tiny bit, an unnoticeable amount. It was only when he suddenly woke up a few months down the track and saw how slipshod the whole outfit had become that he even realized what had been happening.

He grimaced as he strode into the officers' mess tent. He'd gotten as lazy as the rest of them.

But he would be lazy no longer.

Beatrice was waiting for him in England. He had something worth fighting for, worth living for. Someone to come home to.

For her sake, and for the sake of his men, he would work them all until they dropped.

The officers' batman met him at the door, a tray in his hand. "A shipment arrived today, sir. I believe there was a letter for you in the pile."

His heart in his throat, he rifled through the letters on the silver tray, feeling a triumphant smile cross his face when he spied her handwriting.

He had a letter from Beatrice. She had replied to him, and by the weight of the paper it was no brief scrawled note, but a wonderfully long missive full of heart and soul.

Suddenly the weariness of the day left him and he no longer felt the discomfort of his damp clothes or the sunburn on his neck and cheeks. He felt ten foot tall and ready to conquer the known world.

He grabbed the letter and carefully slit open the seal with the letter knife. Then, ignoring his fellow officers' calls to join him at the table, he hunkered down in the corner of the officers' mess and began to read.

Four

Westminster, London, August 1880

Dearest Percy,

    Oh, what I would give to lie under the stars with you. I can see us now, our bodies close, sharing warmth while we gaze into the blazing heavens. How primeval that would be, to do as our distant ancestors did and find stories of bravery and love among the constellations.

    High overhead at the moment is the star Vega, one of the brightest in the sky and part of Lyra, the lyre, an instrument played so beautifully by Orpheus that savage beasts were soothed into placidness (I am fortunate that father insisted on a wide education for me!).

    Our hands are entwined as we talk of the lives of those old Gods, of their wicked ways and their meddling in human affairs. We laugh as our imaginations run wild, each of us making up stories as wild and saucy as those of Zeus and his many consorts and offspring.

    It seems quite natural and comfortable when I move closer to you, my head resting on your chest with your arm around me.

The air is becoming chill with a light dew forming yet we refuse to move. I can hear the beating of your heart, I can feel your breathing as my hand caresses your chest.

It frustrates me so that our clothes are keeping us apart, it would be so wonderful to have your skin next to mine. Then we would truly be like our cave-living ancestors, with nothing around us but nature, a warm fur to keep away the chill, and no one to admonish us for being improper.

The stars wheel overhead in their timeless paths. We sleep, close, until wakened by the first birds of the dawn.

I shall sleep now, hoping for such a dream. Write to me soon.

Love,

Beatrice

P.S. Percy, my love. Be your boldest in your reply. Hold nothing back.

Beatrice lingered over the letter she had just received in reply to her last from Captain Carterton. She could not possibly take it down to share with the others, as had become their habit over the last few months since they had started writing to the soldiers over in South Africa. It was so much more personal than any of the letters the girls had received from the other soldiers. They wrote of the dust and the dirt, of the boredom of having little to do in a country that didn't want them to be there. They wrote of blazing sun and of card games in the mess, and of the loneliness that engulfed them when night fell.

Temptation

But Captain Carterton wrote of his dreams, of his feelings, of the things that mattered to him. Though she knew his words of love and desire were born out of loneliness and fantasy rather than from any true feeling for her, still his language was more than warm, it was positively scorching. It would be a breach of confidence to share any of his words, even the innocuous ones, with the other girls.

Bronkhorstspruit, Transvaal, September 1880
Dearest Beatrice,

My heart increased apace when I received the envelope contain-ing your last letter, but my, when I got to your postscript my breath stopped for an eternity. I have been wanting to write all my thoughts to you, but I had barely the courage to think such thoughts of you, let alone to put my desires into words.

Many a night I lie in my tent, wondering what you look like in your undergarments. I know it is wrong of me, but a soldier must take his amusement where he can. You are an educated woman, a nurse, and I am sure you have anatomical knowledge of what happens when a lonely man thinks such thoughts.

I feel compelled to put my desires and fantasies to paper, as I do not know if this will be my last letter to reach you for some time. Perhaps it will be the last I shall ever write in my lifetime. The Boers here are getting a bit restless, and I fear we may soon see a skirmish or two. You must forgive me, my darling, if my words are too strong. I hope and pray they do not offend you.

Last night was typical of the lonely nights here. The nights are reasonably warm, and I lie on my stretcher with just a blanket for bedding. Can you imagine me lying there? I have removed my uniform and hung it carefully from the tent pole. Being an officer I have a tent of my own and I stand naked in the cooler evening air without fear of interruption from my men.

I squint, and in my mind's eye I can see you sitting on the edge of my stretcher in the darkness, looking at my nakedness. Already I am getting hard at the thought of lying next to you. I lie down under the coarse blanket and pushing it to the side think of your warm smooth skin next to mine instead. We are in England, where our touching is accompanied by the hoot of the tawny owl, rather than the growl of the night-hunting leopard, which is all too common here.

I can feel your breasts, soft to the touch but with hard nipples erect with arousal. As am I. Your belly rises and falls with your breathing, and you squirm slightly when I tickle you in your navel. You stop the tickling by pushing my hand lower where I rest my hand in the tangle of your soft hair.

Now I can feel your hand sliding across my leg seeking my desperate cock. Starting slowly you slide your hand up and down, full strokes that leave me straining for control after only a few moments. Desperately my fingers seek your moist pussy to return the pleasure. Feeling your warm wetness sends me over the edge and my cock spurts across my stomach and chest. Feeling this you cry out with your own pleasure, my fingers become drenched with your climax.

Then my dream ends and I return to the reality of the Transvaal, my seed cooling on my body. I clean up with a cloth,

*cover myself with my blanket, and fall asleep with the thought
of you next to me, the smell of your hair and the sound of your
breath vivid in my mind. What a wonderful sleep!*

*My darling Beatrice—it is now two days since I wrote these
words. I am scared to send them, what will you think? Some de-
praved monster that needs to be locked away? What if the army
censors read my letter? I care not what they think, but I do care
for you. I hope you will read my letter and think of me as a lonely
soldier 6,000 miles from home, thinking of you not just with the
passion of a lonely man, but with true love.*

*I shall send it! Then the die is cast. You will either reply or
not. I hope you do.*

With love,

Percy

She refolded his letter and put it away at the back of her desk
drawer where no one could possibly chance on it. He must be a
true rake to write such words to her, but she couldn't deny that
they heated her blood. He described lying with a woman, with
her, as pleasure not as a sin.

She wondered if she would dare to reply to him in the same
vein . . .

Six or seven of the other girls were already gathered around
the table in the parlor. She drew up a chair and joined the
group. They did not even notice she came empty-handed.

"My soldier is asking for a photograph," one of them said
excitedly, waving her letter in the air. "He says he wants to

see what his lady correspondent looks like. Do you think I should send him one? I could have a sixpenny tintype taken by the photographer who comes to the park every Sunday." She turned her head to look out of the window. "He is probably still there now. I could find him if I hurry."

"Are you sure that's a good idea?" another girl ventured quietly. "He might come looking for you when he gets back home. Do you want to be courted by a poor soldier on half-pay?"

The first girl's enthusiasm wasn't quenched. "I'm sure I wouldn't mind if he did want to court me."

Beatrice was silent as the argument raged around her, lost in thought. Should she send a picture of herself to Captain Carterton, as he had asked her to? On the whole, she didn't think so. She was still walking out with Dr. Hyde. Not that you could call him her sweetheart, exactly, their relationship was too rational and platonic for such an emotional term. Still, she didn't want the captain to know her as anything other than words on a piece of prettily scented stationery. He was her fantasy; he had no place in the reality of her life. She wasn't sure why she balked at the thought of sending him a picture, except that it would make their correspondence seem too real.

It was a pity that her relationship with the captain, if you could call an exchange of letters a relationship, was a hundred times more affectionate than Dr. Hyde's tepid courtship. The captain's letters were so much more intelligent and full of personal insight than Dr. Hyde's conversation. So much warmer and more loving. So much more appreciative of her as a woman.

And so much more inclined to make her think of deliciously intimate pleasures.

Captain Carterton had turned out to be a man of more substance than she had thought at first. He was clearly well educated and interesting, with a turn of phrase that could heat any young woman's blood. If she were to meet him in society, they might even become friends. Or more . . .

"Of course you should send him a photograph if you want to," Mrs. Bettina said stoutly, putting an end to the argument. "There's nothing wrong with writing to a lonely soldier, and no harm in sending him a picture. A modest picture, of course."

"I'm not so sure about that," one of the others said darkly. "Don't we all know what he wants to do with a photograph of a pretty girl. The saucier it is, the better he'll like it." She made an obscene gesture with one of her hands to make it quite clear to what she was referring.

The girls all laughed, and some of them, Beatrice among them, blushed. It seemed somehow wrong to think of the soldiers off fighting for their country as . . . as doing *that*, just as if they were grubby schoolboys.

But when Captain Carterton described it to her in his letters, he made it sound so delightful, as if bringing himself to orgasm while thinking of her was an act of love for her. She liked to imagine him lying in his tent, one hand stroking his stiff cock while the other held a picture of her. It made her want to do just the same, only with a picture of him.

Maybe she would send him a photograph of herself after all.

A saucy one. And ask him to send her his likeness in return. What Dr. Hyde didn't know wouldn't hurt him.

"They are all alone by themselves out in South Africa, after all," one of the girls pointed out. "Without any English girls to keep them company."

"Not that we'd help them out in that regard, even if we were there with them," another said, her voice a bit tart. She had a reputation on the ward as being a bit of a tease. "A prick-tease," Beatrice had heard her referred to as once by a disgruntled patient, a vulgar young bricklayer who'd wanted more from her than nursing.

"They can't have much else to do, stuck in a dusty, hot place without any society."

"We'd be doing a public service by helping them out. And it's not as if it will hurt us. Or our reputations. We can't help that men have baser needs."

"Let's all get tintypes done. We can ask the photographer man to come by when he is finished at the park. A few photos of each of us will make it worth his while. And keep the soldiers as happy as pigs in mud."

Mrs. Bettina was the only one who demurred at the suggestion. "I do not think the sergeant-major would appreciate a photo of an old widow." She heaved a sigh that spoke of wasted opportunities and regrets. "He would not be interested in my letters if he were to know how old I am."

"You are not yet forty," Beatrice protested. "And by his own account he is nearing fifty."

Mrs. Bettina wasn't convinced. "Women lose their looks sooner than men do. I am past being able to find another husband even were I to want one, but if he were to start looking for a wife he'd find himself a young girl of twenty who'd be glad to take him. Respectable men with an honorable profession are not two a penny."

"He's not looking for a wife—just a letter," Lenora pointed out with unassailable logic.

"If it matters so much to you, send him a photograph of one of us instead," one of the other girls put in. "As you said yourself, there's no harm in innocently keeping a man happy."

Mrs. Bettina allowed herself to be persuaded to at least consider the idea, and a couple of the girls ran off to the park to beg the photographer to pay them a visit on the promise of at least a score of tintypes to be taken.

In the resultant shuffle, Beatrice found herself sitting on the couch with Lenora.

"What has your soldier written to you this week?" Lenora asked with a smile of complicity at the game they were playing. "Mine writes of nothing interesting, except that he wishes I was there to keep him company. I doubt it would do him much good if I was—he is not the most articulate of correspondents and would doubtless be a dull companion. He's not educated like Dr. Hyde, and he has no idea of wit or humor. But he was grateful for the socks I knitted him, so I am glad to be of some use."

Beatrice shifted uneasily in her seat. Poor Lenora was too

unworldly to hide her feelings. She was happily oblivious to the fact that all of the hospital knew of and pitied her for her unrequited affection for the doctor. Everyone liked Lenora too much to embarrass her by telling her that her secret was common knowledge.

Beatrice did not want to rub her friend's nose in the doctor's clearly expressed partiality for her. "You could liven your soldier up a bit," she suggested, partly to take Lenora's mind—and her conversation—off the doctor for once. "Get him thinking about you in a whole new way, and see what flights of fancy you can inspire him to."

Her forehead creased into a frown and she crinkled her freckled nose with puzzlement. "But how?"

Beatrice sighed. Lenora did not have a single coquettish bone in her body. Everything about her was completely open and honest. Which was all very well except when it came to the male sex. They liked a little mystery in their women—it added to the allure. "Maybe just a little hint of how lonely you are without him. How you lie awake in bed at night thinking of him."

"But I don't. Not of him," she added, giving away her ill-kept secret all over again.

"I didn't say you had to write him the truth. Embellish it a little. Be just a little bit saucy and see how he responds." It wouldn't hurt to give Lenora a few tips on how to flirt with a young man. If anyone needed them, Lenora did.

Lenora worried her bottom lip with her teeth. "I am not

sure that I know how to be saucy. I'm not sure I even want to know."

"Of course you do. Every woman does. That's how we get men to be interested in us. They like to be led on just a little, and then have us draw back. Show them that we want to be caught, but refuse to come to their bait. It's the not knowing whether we are serious or not that keeps them dangling."

"Is that how you attracted Dr. Hyde?"

Beatrice nodded. One of these days she would have to hint to Lenora that her interest in the doctor was horribly, painfully, obvious. She wasn't in the slightest jealous of the doctor's attention, but she did not want anyone poking fun at her friend for her undisguised adoration of a man who was so clearly indifferent to her. "Of course."

Lenora squared her shoulders. "I shall try, then. But what shall I say?"

Beatrice turned to the rest of the girls in the room. "Ideas, please. What should Lenora say to entice her soldier?"

"Not too much," Lenora added hastily. "Just a little bit. So he doesn't think I am a dry stick."

"Pretend you are in love with him and say what comes naturally."

"But I am not in love with him. Not at all."

"That's why I said *pretend*, silly."

Lenora's face splotched with fiery red. "Oh, I see," she mumbled. "But even if I were in love with him, which I'm not, I still don't know what I should say."

"Oh heavens, have you never whispered silly nothings into a man's ear at night, after he has taken you to a show? Nonsense stuff that you don't mean and which means nothing, but which he wants to hear?"

"Like what?"

"Like how his nearness makes your heart beat faster."

"Or how his kiss makes you go weak at the knees."

"That you will count every second until you can see him again."

"And if you live to be one hundred, you will not forget him."

"He'll be eating out of your hand and begging you for more in no time."

Still Lenora hesitated. "It hardly seems fair to the poor man, writing words that I do not mean."

Myrtle, a hard-bitten woman who wore a look of perpetual disappointment like a badge of honor, let out a burst of bitter laughter. "What's sauce for the goose, dearie. What's sauce for the goose. You don't think that any of them mean a word of what they write to us, now?"

Just then the other girls came back, photographer in tow. "Photograph time," they cried in unison. "Line up for a photograph to send to your sweetheart."

The photographer set up his camera and tripod at one end of the bay window, where the light was best, and placed a chair at the other end. "Now then, ladies," he called out in his cheerful salesman patter, "who's first?"

Myrtle was the first to plump herself down in the chair. "Now then, dearie," she said to the photographer, "make me look pretty, or I shan't pay up." There was enough steel in her voice to make the threat real.

The photographer opened his eyes wide in mock horror. "How could I make you look anything else," he exclaimed, quickly taking an exposure while Myrtle's mouth was still curved in a genuine smile.

She looked critically at the image as it appeared on the thin sheet of japanned iron. "I like it. Take another one."

As he varnished the first print with a few deft brushes, Myrtle removed the black fichu from her bodice and tugged it down to expose her ample bosom. Then she arranged herself in the chair, artfully pulled up her skirts to show her petticoats and more than a hint of ankle, and leaned forward with a pout.

The photographer took another exposure, and the grinning Myrtle gave her place to the next in line.

"You're not going to send that one to your soldier friend, are you?" Mrs. Bettina asked anxiously as the photograph was developed.

"Never you mind what I want it for," Myrtle snapped back. "That's my business."

Beatrice and the others peeped at the image to see what Mrs. Bettina was fussing about. There was a chorus of oohs and aahs as they saw the finished tintype. Myrtle, hard-faced Myrtle, looked like a siren.

"You look so glamorous," Lenora breathed. "So worldly and sophisticated. Do you think he could take one of me looking like that?"

"You look quite improper," Mrs. Bettina said with a sniff. "You don't look like the sort of lady who works as a nurse in London's best hospital."

Myrtle tucked the finished tintypes away in her pocketbook with a smug look on her face. "Good. I don't want to look like a nurse."

Neither did Beatrice, if the alternative was looking as good as Myrtle. She vowed to show off as much bosom and ankle as Myrtle had, or more. If Captain Carterton was going to get an illicit thrill out of looking at her, she may as well give him an eyeful.

One by one, all the girls copied Myrtle's pose, getting more and more outrageous with every photograph that was taken, until Myrtle crowned the joke by pulling her skirts so high to show off her garter, and her bodice so low as to expose one dusky nipple.

"That's quite enough." Mrs. Bettina clapped her hands together and shooed the photographer out the front door as soon as the last tintype was developed and varnished. "You have gone too far."

Myrtle just gave her a saucy wink. "I did this one especially for you, dearie. To send to your sergeant-major. You can pretend it's you, and he'll never know the difference. See if he doesn't write back to you a hundred times over with that sort of promise to keep him dangling."

"I shall do no such thing," Mrs. Bettina huffed. "It would be quite scandalous."

But Beatrice was almost certain she could see the glint of excited temptation lurking in the corner of their landlady's eye.

Nancy Bettina stayed in the parlor long after the younger girls had gone to bed. The coal fire had long since died down into a heap of embers. Though the glowing red coals had dulled into a mass of crumbling gray, they still gave off a pleasant warmth. She drew her chair closer to the fire, pulled up her skirts a little ways and stuck her toes close to the fire to catch every last bit of heat.

From her pocket she drew out the letter she had received from Sergeant-Major Tofts. She had not shared it with the other girls. They were so much younger than she was, and might look oddly at her if they knew how strongly a woman's heart beat under her bodice.

Dear Mrs. Bettina,

Thank you so much for your letter, and your kind thoughts. I must say I was dashed surprised to get a parcel from England, yours is the first I have received since stepping ashore in this place so far from home.

The socks fit me wonderfully and are very comfortable in both the heat of the day and in the chill of the night. You are indeed a generous soul to put so much effort into a gift for a complete stranger.

Allow me to allay your fears of large carnivores gobbling men at every opportunity. I have yet to see a lion or a jaguar, although I do hear them at night on occasion. They are nocturnal hunters you know, but do not bother us as long as we remain in our tents. As for spiders, I too have a slight aversion to them. Nasty creatures, why ever God put them on this earth is beyond me. I pray of you, keep this information to yourself, if ever my men discovered this weakness I am sure they would think the lesser of me.

I believe I would have got on famously with your sadly departed husband, George. When it comes to a man's weapon, cleanliness is next to godliness. I shudder to think of my trusty Martini Henry misfiring at an inopportune moment, just when my life depended on it. Sand and grit are the real enemy here and I, along with my men, spend several hours each day cleaning and oiling our rifles. Not too much oil, mind, as oil is a dirt-magnet. But just enough to keep the parts sliding smoothly and the rust at bay.

You are right in your letter that we are of similar occupation, as I also have the welfare of my men at heart. I find I have to run a tight operation, with the maintenance of discipline being paramount to our survival in this hostile place so far from home. Despite my men considering me a gruff old soldier I feel we must be of closer spirit than you suspect.

I would be honored if you would write again, and if fate and chance permit maybe one day we shall meet in person and I will be able to thank you in person for your uncommon kindness. If I may be so bold, I will hold you in my mind as a strong and intel-

ligent woman, as having a vision helps me get through the long days. And nights.

Warmest regards,
Sgt. Maj. Bartholomew Tofts, V.C.

She put it aside again with a sigh. Though she had been widowed for the better part of a decade, she was only thirty-eight. She still had so much life to live, and it made her weep to think she would spend it all alone. It wasn't fair that the sergeant-major was considered in the prime of his life, ripe for marriage and a family, while she was considered too old. And she and her first husband had never been blessed with children of their own.

She wiped a melancholy tear away. It was too late for her now. Best that she simply accept it and move on with her life. The young nurses that boarded with her were her family. They would have to suffice her.

In a letter, though, she could pretend she was still a young woman. She could pretend that the sergeant-major was her sweetheart and that he was courting her. His letters gave her something to look forward to, something extra to live for, a reason to keep on with the struggle instead of giving up and letting the cares of the world overwhelm her.

They had so much in common, and he wrote so sensibly of matters. Sometimes he reminded her quite forcibly of her late husband. He had the same forthright spirit. The same manly strength and the same uncomplaining nature.

Or maybe it was the loneliness of her heart that made her cling to the first respectable man who had shown any interest in her for a very long time.

She had had her fair share of offers from less than respectable men. The young rag-and-bone man who tried his best to flirt with her every week was one such. Dirty and ill-educated, he clearly saw her—an older woman presumably desperate for a husband—as an easy route to a comfortable bed every night and plenty of hot water.

The sergeant-major wasn't interested in her comfortable boardinghouse or the nest egg she had saved for her later years. He didn't know she was comfortably off, that her dear George had left her so. He wrote to her because he enjoyed her conversation.

If he were to lose interest in their correspondence, her heart would be shattered all over again.

Myrtle's naughty tintype lay on the side table where she had deliberately left it to tempt Mrs. Bettina into sending it to her sergeant-major.

She picked it up and examined it carefully. Myrtle looked very enticing, but she was clearly not in the first flush of youth. Would the sergeant-major be more tempted to carry on their correspondence if he thought she looked like young Myrtle?

It would be a deception if she were to send it to him, but a harmless one. They would never meet in person for him to find her out. He would never know that her hair was not raven black but a soft brown just starting to go gray at the edges, that her waist was no longer quite as slender as it was, and her bosom was far more rounded than it had a right to be. He would not see that she was shy about her no-longer-youthful body, but would think she was brave and bold like Myrtle. Bold enough to show the man she fancied what she wanted, and to lead him on to give it to her.

And it gave her a secret thrill to think she would be fueling his fantasies, that he would be thinking of her as he lay in his tent at night, all alone save for the night birds and insects. For sure the rag-and-bone man didn't think of her at night. Doubtless he spent his evenings in a dark alley with a drunken sixpenny whore, shoving his hands down her bodice and up her skirts, taking his pleasure from her roughly, little caring whether he hurt her or no.

The sergeant-major would have more class than that. He would treat his woman with love and tenderness.

Not that she would ever find out, of course. Still, it would do no harm to pretend for a while longer.

Shaking her skirts back down over her ankles, she moved over to the writing table and picked up pen and paper. She would send him a short note to go with the tintype, and hope for the best.

Five

Percy Carterton sat in his tent, writing as hastily as he could. They had received the orders at dinner, shortly after the last packets had arrived, that they were to move out in the morning. To his delight, there had been another letter for him from England, along with a precious photograph of the woman he adored.

In the haste to get mobilized, he'd barely had the time to skim read the letter he carried in his pocket, but the few stolen minutes had been enough to put a bright song into his heart.

His darling Beatrice had replied to his last letters, and with words as warm as any lover could desire. With every line they exchanged, he fell more deeply in love with her—with her courage, her dedication to those in need, and her passion. Especially with her passion. Her latest letter was burning a hole in his pocket, it was so hot.

Though their mobilization orders had been urgent, he stole

enough time from his preparations to reply. He could not have her thinking that he did not care for her, or that he had been shocked by the warmth of her words. Quite the opposite. They had given him heart for the battle that was to come.

His commanding officer was shouting orders outside. He scrawled a loving farewell to his Beatrice, sealed the letter, and made for the officers' mess. Darkness had already fallen, but the full moon lit up the campsite better than a dozen lanterns. "See this gets to England," he said to the officers' batman, thrusting the letter into his hand.

The batman stopped in his tracks and gave him an alarmed look. "But—?"

"Don't ask me how. Just do it." And he strode off again, his boot heels clacking together. Willis was a resourceful fellow. If anyone could see that his letter got to its destination, Willis was the man.

The following morning, Percy marched across the dusty ground at the head of his company of men. His stride was as jaunty as a cock robin's. After months of simmering tensions since England had annexed the Transvaal, the Boers had finally responded by coming out in open rebellion against the new government. It was finally time to show these upstart Boers who was really in charge.

The sooner they engaged with the enemy, the better he would like it. He would fight this war and win it, and return to England as the proud victor, the captain of a brave troop of soldiers. As soon as he returned to England, he would find his angel and claim her as his own. She would be powerless to resist him, indeed, she would have no will to resist him, longing for him as ardently as he longed for her.

He could tell from her letters that she would be a passionate mistress, bolder and more inventive in bed than many women with more experience than she had. Their hot natures would mesh perfectly together, creating a fiery explosion of desire.

What did he care for the dust turning his white cork hat a dull, muddy brown, and staining the dark blue trousers of his regimentals? The early summer sun was on his back and the wind was in his hair, and he was off to fight for merry England.

The pipe band played merrily as they marched, their cheerful tunes piercing the clear air and carrying across the countryside in a show of defiance. The spirits of all the men in the column were high. Their months of inaction through the winter had told heavily on them, and even the prospect of a new place to camp broke the monotony of their dreary days of waiting.

Three hours later, when the regiment had moved barely a mile down the road, he was less sanguine. The summer sun beat down hot on the dark fabric of his uniform, and his sweat prickled his underarms. Early in the day his horse had taken lame, and he had been forced to dismount and walk at the head of his troops. His boots, better suited for riding than for long marches, had rubbed his heels into blisters. He had even sunk so low as to feel a moment of envy for the uncivilized Boers, who had no uniform but wore clothes of an indeterminate mid brown or gray—light enough to reflect the worst of the sun, and loose enough to breathe.

The pipe band had long since given up playing, and the band members marched along as dully as the rest of the company with their instruments at their sides.

The supply wagons were the worst of their problems. Poorly maintained and worked hard, they were now showing their age. More heavily laden than usual, their lightweight axles could not stand up to the hard ground over which they had to travel. Every time another one broke, the whole column had to stop and cool their heels, standing around in the hot sun, until the wagon was repaired.

When the sun finally went down, they had traveled maybe half of the distance to the small encampment they were charged with fortifying. The wagons were brought together into a defensive circle. Inside the circle, the men ate cold rations then unrolled their bedrolls and lay down in the open, without even bothering to pitch a tent. Despite the difficulties of the day, their mood was still light, and snatches of song and ribald laughter carried out over the veld.

Captain Carterton chose a relatively isolated spot for his bedroll right at the edge of the laager, almost under the wagon wheels. Hoping for any measure of privacy was too much, but at least here he had a few yards of space to call his own, and could read over his letter without fear of someone looking over his shoulder.

He unfolded the pages, smoothing out each wrinkle with a

careful hand. The moon was nearly full, and bright enough to read by.

Westminster, London, October 1880
My poor lonely Percy,

I have read your letter over and over again. Never has anyone written or spoken such words to me, and I had no idea to what extent such words would play on my feelings. Reading your words I can see so clearly you lying in your tent thinking of me. My skin warms and my heart races in my chest with the thought of being so vivid in your imagination.

But how can I reply to such a letter? As you say, the die is cast, and I see no reason to hold back now. If I had been offended you would not have received this letter. And how could I reply with idle chatter of cricket or of the weather when your words were so full of physical love?

There is only one way. I am sitting at my desk and my hand is shaking ever so slightly as I write. I am alone, with my roommate halfway into her shift. No one will disturb me as I write to you.

In my letter I will enclose a photo of me, but all you can see is my face atop a volume of clothing. In the photo you can see my hair is dark. In fact it is a light brown, and my eyes are green. Look at that photo and now in your mind remove all that clothing, layer by layer. First you will discover rather utilitarian undergarments, but always clean and white. And underneath that you will find not the chubby body of a woman who gossips and does needlepoint all day, nor the scrawniness of someone mal-

nourished, but the slightly stocky frame of a woman who works all day as a nurse.

My shoulders are perhaps broader than most women from good nourishment and the physical labor of lifting patients. My breasts are smaller than many. You stare at my nipples, which become small hard points of pleasure, and are quite pink with the flush of your attentions.

Lower down, the soft hair that you so gently run your fingers through, is also a light brown and quite sparse. If you opened this letter carefully, and I hope you have, you will have found a small lock of hair, quite short with a tight curl. I cut it with love, and hope that it will help you with your thoughts in your next letter.

Although I have slightly stocky shoulders my hips are slim, with buttocks that are firm to the touch.

Last night I lay in my bed, imagining I was in your stretcher in Africa, like in your letter. I could smell the dry grass, the dust of the plains, and your body close by. A wild animal called softly in the night, perhaps a lion or a jaguar. I looked up to watch you undress, silhouetted in the moonlight. Already you are standing proud, your body rampant at the thought of lying next to me.

I confess it is hard to write of such things, but in my mind we are in a primeval place, nature all around, and we are together, man and woman with only canvas to keep nature at bay.

Your cock (there, I wrote it!) was hard and clearly visible against the background light of the tent.

Temptation

As if it had a mind of its own my hand reached out to touch you. I couldn't wait, for yours was the first I have ever touched in a loving way. I hoped you would want me to do that.

Your hand dipped lower and my body arched to give you better access to my secret places while my hand involuntarily squeezed you a bit harder. Unexpectedly you came, spurting your seed over your belly and chest. As you peaked, your hand rubbed harder between my legs and, like you, I was unable to stop the flood of pleasure overwhelming me.

We lay in the cool of the night, the blanket had fallen to the dusty dirt floor unheeded. I watched you fall asleep, kissing you good-night as your breathing slowed to a peaceful rhythm. I pulled the blanket over us and I too fell asleep, the sounds of Africa caressing my mind.

Write soon, my love,
Beatrice

He could almost hear her voice speaking to him through the night, the voice that had helped him to keep his sanity through these long, lonely days in South Africa. Soft and sweet, it had called to him like no other.

How he wished he was alone in his tent and could reach down into his bedroll to stroke the erection that her letter had provoked in him, to think of her standing in the flesh before him, to dream of her sweet body until he massaged himself into a temporary oblivion. But his neighbors were too close for comfort, and he had no wish to be caught out like a schoolboy.

Instead, he gritted his teeth and willed his rampant body to subside.

Despite his tiredness, and the prospect of another long and frustrating march in the morning, it was a long time before he could settled down comfortably enough on his bedroll to go to sleep. Even when he finally dropped off, it was only to dream of Beatrice.

He woke with the sun, feeling washed out and wretched after a night of fruitless fantasies. It was easier to dream of Beatrice and to imagine that she was close by him when the sun was gone from the sky and all was dark around him. In the harsh glare of the day, he could not conjure up her image so easily. The illusion that he could almost reach out and touch her faded in the heat and the sunshine.

The trumpeter played a drowsy reveille, and all around him the men started to wake up, turning over in their bedrolls and rubbing sleep out of their eyes. He was already up and had shaken the worst of the dust off his bright red jacket and pulled it on over his rather crumpled linen. He made a face at the sweat and grime that already dirtied it. There would be no clean clothes until they reached the new campsite, and at their slow pace it could take them another day or more.

He splashed a little water on his face and hands from his canteen just to refresh himself. Thank heavens Beatrice could not see him now, unwashed and covered in dust. She might change her mind about him and decide that a rough-and-ready soldier was not to her taste after all.

The fleeting thought brought a smile to his face. He was not worried about Beatrice's fidelity—hadn't she stayed his faithful correspondent these many months?

Breakfast was cold rations again. The company commander did not want to linger to make a fire to heat their food. The men grumbled a little, but subsided when Percy reminded them that the sooner they left, the sooner they would make it to the camp, where there would be hot food aplenty and decent lodgings once more.

This time the pipe band didn't play quite so jauntily as they set off once more. Cold beef jerky and a lump of bread for dinner at night and then again for breakfast the next morning would dampen anyone's enthusiasm for music-making.

Percy felt no more like singing than the rest of the company. Though he had padded his feet with strips of linen torn off a spare shirt, still the blisters on his heels smarted with every step he took. And with every step that he took, his rage against the Boers, who had dragged them into this conflict with their refusal to accept British sovereignty, grew. Had it not been for their intransigence, he would be home in England, with Beatrice as his wife and a brood of children on the way.

A home. A family of his own. It was strange how the attraction for such things had grown on him over the last year. Eighteen months ago he would have run screaming from the prospect of a wife and children. Now it was all he wanted out of life.

Just before noon there was a commotion in the ranks ahead

of them. Squinting into the distance, Percy caught sight of a plume of dust rising from the veld. It wasn't large enough for a column of men, just half a dozen riders riding toward them.

As they came closer, Sergeant-Major Tofts turned to him with a sniff. "Boers, by the look of them. I'd recognize their slouch hats anywhere." He patted his own cork hat with a measure of self-satisfaction. "You can always recognize the quality of your opponent by the quality of his headgear."

Percy narrowed his eyes against the sun. "What do they think they are doing, riding up to the column of English troops in broad daylight?" Surely the six of them could not be thinking of mounting some kind of resistance. It would be little more than suicide for a handful of lone men to pit themselves against the might of an English regiment.

The sergeant-major shrugged. His bushy moustache was thick with dust, the same dust that had stuck to the sweat on his face and made him look almost as brown as a Zulu. "Damned if I can read their mind. They're not Englishmen. They don't think like we do."

The regiment kept on marching as the men approached. The lone riders did not stop until they were directly in the regiment's path, blocking their way. Awkwardly, the regiment shuffled to a halt.

"This is Boer land," the foremost of the riders called. He did not stammer or look intimidated at the might of the English soldiers in front of him. Percy was just forward enough in the column to hear every word carried clearly through the air.

Lieutenant-Colonel Anstruther, the commander of their regiment, riding at the head of the column, drew himself to his full height and looked down his nose at the shabbily clad riders in front of him. "We are in British territory. I have a right to pass with my men." He looked, Percy thought, like a turkey cock, pompously gobbling his indignation at being accosted in such a fashion.

The leader of the Boer party gave a grim smile. Even at this distance, Percy could see the tension in his bearing. Every muscle in his body looked as though it was on high alert, poised for action. "If you advance any further, it will be construed as an act of war." For all they were a small party of men, it was abundantly clear they were in deadly earnest.

Anstruther was not impressed by their threats. "I refuse to bow down to the ridiculous demands of a scruffy little would-be militia."

"I am warning you, we will take every measure necessary to defend ourselves against what we consider an act of aggression."

"I repeat, this is British territory, and I shall travel where I please."

"Then the blood of your men will be on your hands." With that parting shot from their leader, the group of riders wheeled away and rode off.

Percy watched them carefully as they rode away, the plume of dust that marked their passage disappearing every so often into the hollows of the undulating landscape.

The veld was not as flat as it appeared at first sight, but marked with small rises and falls, almost unnoticeable to the casual observer.

Percy had scarcely noticed the dips in the ground as he was walking, but watching the riders disappear and then reappear as they rode away made his belly feel as though he had eaten a plateful of live snakes for breakfast. "If you knew the country well, you could fit a whole regiment alongside the road within firing distance, and no one would suspect a thing," he muttered uncomfortably to the sergeant-major walking alongside him.

Even now they could be surrounded by enemies and walking straight into a trap, oblivious of the danger they faced. His instincts were telling him that something was very wrong.

The sergeant-major caught the direction of his gaze and nodded. "You're right. I don't like it any more than you do. The whole thing smells a bit odd to me. I don't trust them Boers further than I could kick 'em."

Sometimes all a soldier had to go on were his instincts. Percy swung on to the back of his horse. Despite the weeping blisters on his own feet, he'd been leading his mare all day to give her foot a rest, but her lameness seemed to have disappeared as quickly as it had developed. Shaking her reins, he encouraged her into a fast trot until he came level with the lieutenant-colonel.

He saluted his superior officer. "Sir, would you like me and my men to ride ahead as a scouting party? That way we'll be able to see any trouble that might be out there before the entire regiment is caught up in it."

Anstruther peered down his nose as if he were examining a speck of dung on his boot, and made a dismissive gesture with one hand. "The land is as flat my mother-in-law's chest. If the Boers try anything foolish, we shall see them come riding up to us from a mile away."

"But—"

Anstruther cut him off before he could finish pointing out that the ground was deceptively uneven. "Boers got you rattled, have they?" he asked condescendingly.

Percy was too angry at the insinuation that he was a coward to reply.

"There's no need to worry about them," Anstruther continued, quite oblivious to Percy's fury. "They are like the toothless old collie dog I left in England—their bark is worse than their bite. They'll soon learn we're wise to their bluster."

"And if they take advantage of the uneven ground and attack?"

"Then we fight them off. We have ten times their firepower. They are no match for a well-trained group of Englishmen." He gave Percy a barely veiled look of disdain that indicated how little he thought of his junior officer's fears. "Now, off into line with you."

Percy saluted slowly, wondering how he could convince the lieutenant-colonel that real danger lay ahead of them. As an English officer, he could not disobey a direct order from his commander, but every nerve in his body screamed that they were heading into a trap. "If you are quite sure that the Boers have no plan whatsoever behind their bravado," he said stoutly, "then I will be happy to fall back into line at your express order."

The older man paused for a moment at the hint of insubordination in his tone and gave a brief glance at the road in front of him. Then he sat up fractionally straighter on his horse, a slight frown creasing his brow. "I suppose it would do no harm to give the order for the ammunition to be passed out before we continue our march. It will give the men confidence and cheer their spirits to think they might have a chance to engage with the enemy."

That was at least something, though not the order to take out a scouting party that he had been hoping for. He saluted again, rather more smartly this time, and kicked his mare into a trot.

The ammunition wagon was toward the middle of the column, where it could easily be protected if they were surprised. The company quartermaster grumbled morosely as he wrestled the heavy covers off the wagon. "Four hours time and all this lot will have to be put back again. I wonder if the colonel thought of that when he gave the orders to unpack it all."

"I expect he thought more about the danger his soldiers could face if they were to cross the veld without any bullets in their guns," Carterton said, in a voice that showed how little he thought of the man shirking in his duty.

The quartermaster muttered a few curses under his breath about goddamned officers sitting up on their high horses and expecting foot soldiers to do all the work, but there was little heat in his words. Despite his grumbling, he had the covers off the wagons as smartly as any commanding officer could wish, and was handing out the rifles with an ease born of long practice.

Even so, a good half hour had passed before the column of troops was once more underway.

Carterton swung back into line with the sergeant-major. His mare was favoring one of her hind legs once more. With a sigh, he reminded himself that the welfare of an officer's horse came before his own comfort. He dismounted, grimacing as his feet hit the packed earth with a thud that scraped needles of pain across his heels. Yesterday's march had been long and painful. Today's was going to be worse.

Walking on and on, across a never-ending plain, put his mind to sleep. His feet followed the steps of the man in front of him without him consciously willing them to while his mind drifted off into a waking dream. Once the war in South Africa was over, his regiment would return to England, victorious.

He would marry Beatrice as soon as he could arrange for the banns to be read. As his wife, the wife of an officer, she would be able to follow the regiment when they were next posted out of England. In addition to his captain's pay, he could, if he chose, draw a significant income from the family's estate. He had taken pride in accepting nothing from his brother all these years—not even what he was legally entitled to. Once he was married, that would change. His wife was more important than his pride. Beatrice would not want for anything—he would delight in spoiling her.

Once they were married, he would never have to be parted from her again. They would have a parcel of children, girls as pretty as their mother, and boys with all her courage and dedication . . .

When the first shots rang out over the veld, he did not immediately realize they were under attack. The first thought that crossed his mind was that one of the less disciplined soldiers had spied a buzzard and decided to pick it off to add to his supper that evening. He looked around the men with some irritation, hoping it wasn't one of his who had broken ranks. Such an infraction would have to be punished, and though he knew it was essential to keep order in the ranks, he disliked having to punish the men under his command.

Not until one of the soldiers several paces in front of him staggered in his tracks, gave a gurgle of distress, and dropped to the ground, blood dribbling from the corner of his mouth, did he understand. The man had been shot.

Sweat coated Carterton's hands, making it hard to hold his rifle, and despite the heat, his skin was cold and clammy. The shot had come so unexpectedly, out of nowhere. One moment the man had been walking across the veld with the rest of them, and now he was on the ground.

Carterton stopped dead, his mind refusing to believe what his eyes could see. The man in front of him twitched once, and then lay still. Dead.

It was as he had feared all along—they had walked straight into a trap.

A trumpet blast from the rear of the column sounded an alarm, but the trumpeter was cut off in midblast, his warning ending abruptly when another couple of shots rang out over the veld, finding their targets with unerring accuracy.

Fear hit him with the force of a bayonet to the chest. Were all his hopes and dreams going to end here, on the high veld of South Africa, done to death by a Boer bullet?

"Shoot the bastards," he yelled at his men. He dropped to one knee, bracing his rifle against his shoulder, blinking furiously to get the dust out of his eyes, the dust that was making them water and blurring his vision. "Aim at their hearts. If you're a poor shot, aim at their horses." Damn it, but the trumpeter had been barely out of his teens. Far too young to die in the dirt like a dog.

It was harder to follow his own instructions than he had thought. The Boers had picked a perfect time and place for their ambush. They rode singly, rather than keeping in formation. In their mud-colored clothes, riding dun horses, they merged into the veld as if they were a part of it. He had to squint into the lowering sun to pick them out.

Just as he got one in his sights and pulled the trigger, the bastard would wheel away and his shot would be wasted. Though he was one of the best marksmen in the regiment, the best he could do was to bring down a horse or two, and take their riders out of action that way.

Few of the men under the other captains had the good sense to aim with any care. They were firing volleys into the air in the general direction of the attacking Boers, counting on the frequency and denseness of their fire to thin the number of attackers. But the Boers were already spread so thinly across the vast landscape that such tactics were utterly useless.

Carterton wanted to scream in frustration as volley after volley of British fire slammed harmlessly into the ground, while every Boer bullet found its mark in the heart of a British soldier. "Aim, you fools," he shouted at them until his voice was hoarse. "Don't just shoot. Aim."

It was over almost as soon as it had begun. He had barely drawn half a dozen breaths before three quarters of the British soldiers were dead or dying on the veld, and the white flag was rising from the ruins of what remained.

He dropped his rifle and rose to his feet again, the horror of the massacre around him pulling at his soul. The Boers had picked off those riding horses first—to get rid of the chain of command. Barely a single officer was left standing, and those who were still alive were bleeding from half a dozen wounds.

Beside him, the sergeant-major had sunk to the ground, his face white and etched with pain. One of his legs was bent at an awkward angle beneath him. Young Teddy Clemens was bending over him. "It's broken." His voice was hoarse with gunpowder smoke, and he cleared his throat with an awkward cough. "He needs a surgeon."

Carterton questioned him with a glance, glad to see the lad still on his feet. "And you?"

"Not a scratch on me." The usual laughter in Teddy's voice was absent. "I must have the luck of the devil." He looked up and immediately jumped to his feet, ripping off his jacket as he did so. "You're bleeding."

Carterton looked at the boy in surprise. "I am?" He had not felt a thing while the shooting was in full swing, but now that he looked down at himself; he could see that his right side was covered in blood and his arm felt as though it was on fire.

With deft hands, Teddy tied a tourniquet around his arm to stop the blood flow. "Thank God for Beatrice, who told me what to do about stuff like this," he muttered as he tied it in a tight knot. "Or I wouldn't have had a clue what to do."

Once he was bandaged up and the bleeding had stopped, the two of them splinted the sergeant-major's leg as best they could and half carried, half dragged him to the surgeon's cart. The Boers were too busy looting the supply wagons to pay the survivors of the massacre any heed.

"Take care, old fellow," Carterton said with a cheerfulness he did not feel, as he and Clemens left the sergeant-major in the shade of the wagon with a flask of water. "The surgeon will have you put to rights in no time."

The effort of carrying his friend to the surgeon had caused his arm to start bleeding again. The makeshift bandage Teddy Clemens had tied around him was heavy with blood. Despite feeling dizzy with blood loss, he followed Teddy back out into the heat to see who else of their regiment they could salvage from this bloody disaster of a battle.

So much for their glorious homecoming, Carterton thought savagely to himself later that evening, as he collapsed exhausted on to the ground. Too, too many of his men were dead, and he had done what he could for those who were hurt. It was up to God and the surgeon now whether they died of their wounds or no.

Teddy handed him a canteen of water and he drank it greedily.

The Boers, reluctant to burden themselves with prisoners, had ridden off again, after first plundering the wagons of as much food and ammunition as they could carry and extracting from the severely wounded Lieutenant-Colonel a promise that he would lead no more men into battle with them. Those left alive were not prisoners, but their situation was precarious nonetheless. They had scores of wounded men to transport, little ammunition, and not enough water to last the distance.

Come morning, they would have to bury their dead, load as many of the wounded into carts as they could, and limp back to camp, defeated.

Six

Beatrice twisted her fingers together as she stared down at the letter in front of her. Captain Carterton had written it to her the night before his regiment had been sent away on extended patrol. Both he and Teddy had been on the front for weeks now. Since she had received the letter the evening before, she had been up most of the night, worrying.

News from the front had been reaching England from telegraphed messages sent from South Africa. The news was all bad for the English. One by one, they had lost every battle in which they had been engaged. The casualties on the English side had been horrific. Every day, more telegraphed messages arrived with the names of the dead inscribed in them.

Word was that the Boers had lost barely a handful of men. They were invincible. The best regiments of English soldiers had been set against them, but not all the might of the English regiments could defeat the handful of ragtag Boer farmers.

And both Teddy and Captain Carterton were charged with fighting them.

Would Teddy ever come home, or would he find a grave in the barren South African lands, along with so many of his fallen comrades? And the Captain? Would this be the last letter she ever received from him? Would her fantasies be buried out there in the veld along with his body?

Their names hadn't yet appeared in the lists of the dead, but she hardly dared hope they were still alive. So many new names were added each day. In times of war, the life of a soldier was so precarious.

A tear fell, blurring the ink on the paper in front of her. She blotted it carefully with the tip of her finger. These might be the last words she ever received from the captain. She would not let them be spoiled.

Bronkhorstspruit, Transvaal, November 1880
Dearest, lovely Beatrice,

Truly you have a wonderful spirit to write such a daring letter. I read it every night and every morning, I'm sure I could recite it word for word without a glance if I did not enjoy so much holding in my hands the paper which you yourself have also held.

And the small lock of hair! What a wonderful, wonderful gift. I have carefully placed it in a small envelope that I made especially, and keep it in my breast pocket so that it is directly over my heart. I save it for special occasions when I am alone (I'm sure you know what I mean) and brush my lips with its softness. I imagine I can smell your scent on it, lingering long after it was cut.

It is just past sunset and there is not much light in my tent, my haste and the darkness are combining to cause my penmanship to be not to its usual standard. I fear things are getting a bit sticky here. We have been given orders to pack for a march and assemble in a column at dawn tomorrow. I should be seeing to my men, but I have taken a few moments to scribble a last letter to you, for I do not know the destination of our march, nor do I know for how long we will be absent from our base.

The Boers are making noises of independence and resent our presence. I feel sure there will soon be some sort of uprising where blood will be spilt. I guess that our marching orders were given to neutralize a new Boer threat. Of course we shall win, with our superior tactics and discipline—the Boers are merely a bunch of ragtag farmers with old hunting rifles.

Worry not for me, my love. My rifle is clean and ready, my ammunition pouches are filled with live ammunition, and my kit is packed ready for the morning with your letters safely wrapped in an oilskin cloth. But I do often wonder at the reason we are here.

If it were not for English hubris in claiming this scrubby desert land we would be at home with our families, I am sure. What do we English want with this land? It is fit for nothing, and scarcely allows the Boers, who have made it their home, to maintain a livelihood. If they will attack, we shall repel, and who will be the losers in this? I'll tell you who, it's the mothers and fathers who *lose their sons, and the daughters and sons who lose their fathers. They will be the real losers.*

Centuries ago the Dominican priest Aquinas wrote of three rules for a war to be just. It must be started and controlled by the authority of state, there must be a just cause, and the war must be for good, or against evil. This impending fight (call it a war, for what else is it when men kill each other in large numbers) does not, in my opinion, seem to meet all of Aquinas's rules. We English are fighting for dominion over a wasteland that no one but a people as desperate and unsociable as the Boers could possibly want. How can this then be a just war?

Of course I will do my duty, and fight for Queen and Country, but I cannot help but wonder at the justice and the waste of such actions. Surely diplomacy and negotiation are far cheaper in both money and lives.

Oh, what a depressing line of thought! If this is indeed my last letter for a while then what a miserable one it is! I shall dwell no longer on such negative thoughts, and in my last minutes of private time I shall think of you, of our lives together in a halcyon future.

I dream we are in a comfortable bed, the sheets are in disarray, and the eiderdown has half fallen to the floor. The curtains are open and the warm sunshine falls on our naked bodies. Outside it is a lovely summer morning, the hills are green and the air is peaceful and quiet.

I can't tear my eyes away from you, your eyes are closed and your breasts rise and fall with your soft breathing. But I don't think you are asleep. Earlier you woke me with a kiss to my cock, and I was hard within seconds of your soft mouth engulfing me. I tasted and nuzzled you, and your smell was just as I imagined from that small lock of hair you sent me a lifetime ago.

Alas I must leave my dream there, the light has all but gone and I have things I must do before we march at dawn. By the time you read this it is likely my life will be different. Most probably there will be a battle with the Boers, and most probably I will have killed someone's son, or I will take the life of some poor child's father. But I pray not, and I pray that reason will prevail.

My next letter will tell of a peaceful resolution or of a violent one. Until then I will be thinking of you every hour of every day.

All my love,
Percy

By the time she had finished, her eyes were awash with tears. The sun was bright now, but her spirits were heavy. Wearily, she threw off her dressing gown and put on her uniform. Though she was exhausted in mind and body, there were patients at the hospital who needed her.

Her first patient of the day was a badly burned young man. She put up a screen around him before she pulled back the covers to wash what was left of his mangled body. The poor man deserved some privacy for his hideous burns, received from an accidental blast at a gunpowder factory where he had been working. He had been carried in to the hospital on a makeshift stretcher by his workmates the day before, more dead than alive.

Though her duty was to save lives, she hated having to save

his. He was so badly burned he was unlikely to live for long, and even if he did, his injuries were so severe he would never work again. When he was awake, he moaned with pain and begged to be set free from his suffering. All she could do was give him enough laudanum to dull his pain and to send him off to sleep. At least in his sleep, the pain and horror of his burns was masked from him.

How she hoped that if Teddy or the captain were to die in battle, they would find a swift end. She hoped they would not know such pain, and the agony of knowing that it would end only with their death.

When she was halfway through her task, the screen was moved aside and Dr. Hyde poked his head through. His eyes widened with displeasure when he saw her. "Beatrice, why have you closed the curtains? It is not seemly that you should be alone with a male patient. Particularly not one who is in a state of undress."

She dragged the screen back around her patient again. "He is badly injured and deserves his privacy." She was too tired and overwrought to mince her words. "It is less seemly that he should be exposed to the gaze of whoever passes by."

"Safety in the hospital is paramount. Hiding behind screens is a foolish act, and puts you at unnecessary risk. You could be in danger from him, and no one would see what was happening until it was too late."

Sometimes Dr. Hyde could be so annoying. Annoying and impractical. She wiped a loose strand of hair off her face with the back of her hand. Her shift had barely started and already she was exhausted. "He is badly injured, and what's more, he's taken enough laudanum to knock out an elephant. I am in no danger from him."

He did not back down. "Your reputation is."

"I am a nurse," she snapped. "Of course I see naked men in the course of my duties. I can hardly wash a patient with all his clothes on."

That made him take a step backward. "You should not talk of such matters." His voice, though controlled, vibrated with anger. "It is unseemly in a young woman, even if she is a nurse."

Oh dear, she had really offended him now. She suppressed a sigh. She would have to flatter him and make him feel like a hero again, or he would sulk for a week. "But we are both professionals, aren't we," she said with a tired attempt at a winning smile. "I can say things to you that I would not say in society. You are quite different from the common run of men."

Her words had the desired effect. His face lightened and he gave an almost-smile of approval. "You're right, of course. Doctors have to see the bigger picture. We cannot be bound by the same rules as the rest of society."

"Indeed, no," she agreed, wanting him only to go away so she could carry out her duties in peace.

"You were right to remind me of the special position we hold. I shall leave you to your task. But may I call on you this Sunday afternoon for a walk in the park?"

Beatrice smiled dutifully, though the thought depressed her.

Why couldn't he do something different for a change, instead of being so predictable? "That would be lovely." He took her acquiescence for granted. Couldn't he ask *her* what she wanted to do for a change, instead of expecting her to accede to his wishes all the time?

Dr. Hyde smiled. "I do like to get out of the hospital on Sundays, and be surrounded by fresh, green nature. I'm so glad you enjoy it as I do."

He withdrew his head from the curtain and Beatrice listened to his footsteps walking away down the ward. Ha, if only he knew how much she was bored of the park and had spent all year wanting to go to a comedy musical show instead. But she had never brought up the idea and he had never bothered to ask her what she wanted to do.

He thought she was happy with his choice of amusement, and so he was happy, and even applauded her for her superior tastes that exactly matched his own.

Really, men were so easy to manipulate, and Dr. Hyde, for all his book learning, was easier than most. Being married to him would be easy enough as long as she took the trouble to make him think he was in control.

Easy, but dull. Marriage to him would condemn her to sedately promenading in the park with him every Sunday for the rest of her life. Had she been too hasty in encouraging his courtship?

She sighed and went back to caring for the ruin of the man in front of her.

He was young and had been handsome once, more's the pity. She could trace his once fine features through the ruin of his face. It was so badly maimed now that even his mother would be hard-pressed to recognize him.

If the war in South Africa continued to go badly, there would soon be many more such casualties hitting the hospital for her to care for. Young men with broken bodies and broken minds, reliving their worst moments over again in their nightmares.

Some of the older nurses had told her stories about the men that had come back from the Crimean War. Some of them, though their bodies were unmarked, had damaged souls and would never be the same again. A few had been unable to bear the strain of what they had become, and had done what the enemy had failed to do, and killed themselves.

It was a tragedy, a double tragedy, that even when the war was over, young men continued to lose their lives.

How she hoped neither Teddy nor Captain Carterton were among the dead or wounded in this war they were fighting in South Africa. She was worn out from hoping it. Until yesterday she had consoled herself with the thought they were far away from the fighting and were sitting out the war barricading a fort in relative safety. Now she knew without a doubt they had been given their marching orders.

There had been no point in her writing a reply to the captain's letter—she would not have known where to send it.

Even when she had thought Teddy and the captain were safe, she had scanned the pages of the daily newspapers every evening, hoping to find only the names of strangers in the growing list of soldiers killed in the line of duty. So far, she had been lucky. After receiving yesterday's letter, she was terrified that her luck would not hold.

Her patient groaned, the noise bringing her back to reality. Carefully, she spooned another dose of laudanum into his partly open mouth with shaking fingers, and stroked his throat until he swallowed. Then she pulled the sheet back over him and removed the screen. She had done all she could for that poor man to ease his passing.

There was no use in fretting over what she could not change—it was a foolish indulgence of sentiment and did no one any good.

She would heal where she could, and comfort where she could not heal.

And only hope that death was merciful and passed her loved ones by.

Percy Carterton clambered onto the deck of the ship, then turned and waved with his good arm to the few soldiers who stood on the docks. Only those in his regiment who had remained unscathed were remaining in South Africa, the rest were being sent home to England to recuperate. He was one of the lucky ones—he had walked up the gangway under his own steam, with only an arm in a sling. Most of his comrades, if he hadn't left them buried in the dusty soil of the Transvaal, had been carried on to the ship in stretchers, groaning under the burden of shattered legs or gaping head wounds.

He spied Teddy Clemens on the dock. The boy had Lady Luck in his corner. He'd come through their first encounter without a scratch, and was now joining another regiment that was off to keep the peace in Pretoria. The lad should be safe enough there, whatever happened in the interior.

"Go see my sisters in London," Teddy shouted at him above the din. He could just make out the lad's words over the racket of the docks. "Tell them I miss them, and I'd be coming home, too, if I could."

Carterton waved back in acknowledgment of the boy's request. He had every intention of fulfilling it at the earliest opportunity. Meeting Beatrice was the only good thing that had come out of this blasted war. And now he was going home to claim her.

Beatrice sat on the rug on the grass and picked idly at the daisies. The band in the rotunda played a jolly marching tune, but her spirits did not rise to match the musicians. They remained as wet and downtrodden as the small patch of lawn on which she was perched. She still had heard nothing from Teddy and she was worn out from worrying over him.

Dr. Hyde sat next to her on the rug, his legs stretched out in front of him, pulling uncomfortably at his goatee. His brown pants clung tightly to his thighs, and he had dispensed with formality just enough to take off his jacket and roll up his shirtsleeves. His arms were covered with fine brown hair that looked soft enough to run her fingers through.

He caught her looking at his arms and a slight frown creased his forehead. With a deliberate motion he rolled down his sleeve and refastened the cuffs.

Beatrice's face blazed with a sudden heat. So what if she had been looking at his arms? It was hardly a crime. Anyone would think they were merely casual acquaintances, instead of a couple who had been walking out together for nearly a year now. She wasn't a nun—she was planning to marry the man if he would ever get up the courage to ask her. There would be something wrong with her if she *didn't* want to look at his bare skin when she had the chance.

A shimmer of irritation with him floated down and settled on her shoulders like a dark cloud. He was not usually such a dull companion. Usually his quick wit would allow her to overlook his formal manners and his stiff-rumped propriety. But this afternoon he was so ill at ease that his sharp brain seemed to have turned quite to mush.

Sometimes, when his humor was especially entertaining, she was almost sure that she was on the way to falling in love with him. This afternoon, however, she wasn't sure that she even liked him. It was an uncomfortable way for a woman to feel about her prospective husband.

Dr. Hyde pulled at his goatee again, until Beatrice wanted to slap his fingers away. How could a respectable doctor have such irritating personal habits? He would pull out all the hairs until he had none left, and his goatee was ridiculously sparse to start with. If she were ever to marry him, she would insist that he shave it off. *Before* their wedding night.

If she were ever to marry him? She gave an inelegant snort that caused him to look at her as if she had just sicked up something nasty in the presence of the Queen. Her worry over Teddy must be turning her brain to mush. Of course she was going to marry him. It had been her dream for most of the last year that the revered Dr. Hyde would fall head over heels in love with her and ask her to be his wife. He was a respectable man and a good doctor, and she liked him very well—most of the time, that is.

As his wife, she would be free to continue to work as a nurse until she was to fall in the family way. He approved of women nurses. That in itself was enough to make him stand out from the crowd. Most of his colleagues acted as if they were doing a favor to the women to allow them to work at the hospital, despite the fact that they worked twice as hard for a fraction of the pay.

Though it had taken her months to break through his reserve, their friendship was now reaching a crisis point. As the daughter of a bankrupt and a suicide, she knew just how important it was to be considered respectable. Without it, a woman had less than nothing.

Annoyingly, the way she felt about the doctor this afternoon, she would be quite happy if he were to announce that he had become engaged to the hospital charwoman and was emigrating to Africa to become a missionary. Even if it meant the end to all her dreams.

He cleared his throat awkwardly. The noise was at least as vulgar as her snort had been, but did she glare at him? No, she did not. Her manners were better than his.

"Beatrice—" He stopped speaking and cleared his throat again. "Beatrice, I have something to ask you?"

Had he always been this irritating, and she had just never noticed? Surely not. She must simply be tired and out of sorts. The afternoon sun was too weak to be warm, the grass was too damp to be comfortable, and the wind was too brisk to make sitting outside a pleasure. Even the band was playing out of tune. It was no wonder she was out of patience. "Ask away."

He frowned at her flippant reply. "It is a serious question."

"To which I will give a serious answer." She laid her hand comfortingly on his thigh, feeling guilty for having vexed him yet again. He had been a good friend to her and she ought not take her ill humor out on him.

He picked up her hand in his and held it there. "Beatrice, we have known each other for a year now."

His remark did not call for a reply, so she remained silent.

"From almost the moment I met you, I was impressed with your dedication to your work and your devotion to your patients."

"Thank you," she murmured, feeling more in charity with him. It was always nice to be appreciated.

"And for some time now we have been growing closer."

She smiled at him as if she agreed with his every word. She'd practiced the smile in the mirror in her lodgings until she had it pitch perfect. Men being what they were, she expected to have to use it often.

"We have." She infused the words with the feeling that in doing so, all her dreams had come true. The truth was, they had been getting to know one another at a snail's pace, despite her best efforts to hurry him along. His courting was frustratingly slow and wishy-washy.

Captain Carterton, wherever he was, would not be such a namby-pamby. He was a man of action who would whisk her off to his private harem and make love to her for three weeks on end, given the chance. His last letters had been quite disturbingly warm.

". . . and I have become very fond of you."

His words broke into her daydream about her soldier. When she was married, she wouldn't have time to write to him anymore, even if he were to survive the war. Marriage would truly spell the end of her naughty fantasies, for she would no longer be able to write to him or to receive his letters. "That's nice," she said weakly. It was a pity that marriage would be so restrictive. Writing to the captain and receiving his letters in return had been the highlight of her days.

". . . as I hope you have of me."

"Indeed." His careful manner was hardly conducive to a rhapsody of love from her in return. She wasn't in the mood for rhapsodies anyway.

Married women shouldn't write such familiar letters to men, she knew. Not that unmarried women should write such letters, either, but as an unmarried woman she was more free to please herself. Fornication was only unforgiveable if one was caught out in it, while adultery was always severely frowned upon.

"And I was hoping you would consider doing me the inestimable honor of becoming my wife."

She let out the breath she didn't even know she had been holding. This was the moment she had been waiting for. To her astonishment, she didn't feel overwhelmed by happiness, or passion. She didn't even feel so much as a nervous butterfly in her stomach. All she felt was a vague sense of irritated letdown. Is this all there was to life? Where were the fireworks that Louisa had described to her, the sense of rightness, of inevitability?

She meant to say yes. She tried to say yes, but her mouth refused to form the word. "I don't know what to say."

"You could accept my offer for a start," Dr. Hyde remarked, with a flash of his usual wit returning.

"No." Where had that word come from? She hadn't meant to say that. "I mean, not yet," she said hastily, covering her mistake as quickly as she could. What was wrong with her? She meant to marry the man. She had meant to marry him for months. Why was she getting cold feet just as his had finally started to get warm?

"Not yet?" He raised his eyebrows for an explanation. "Does that mean maybe, or is it a kinder way of saying no?"

She had none to give him. "It's all rather sudden," she lied, not knowing what else to say. "Marriage is such an important step for a woman. I need some time to think about it."

He tugged on his goatee in thought. "That is fair enough.

Come walking with me next Sunday, and let me know your thoughts then." He rose to his feet and held out his hand to assist her from the ground. "Come, I shall escort you back to your boardinghouse."

Beatrice was thankful that she was wearing cotton gloves. Her skin was cold and clammy. It frightened her, how close she had come to throwing away everything she had worked for in the past year.

They walked the two miles back to her boardinghouse in near silence. Clouds covered any hint of sunshine and Beatrice shivered in her light cloak. Her Sunday outing had turned into a disaster. A disaster completely of her own making.

When they reached the door, Dr. Hyde bowed over her hand. "I shall see you on the wards in the morning, I trust?" His words were as courteous as ever, but he looked as sour as if he had eaten a peck of lemons. Sour enough to curdle milk at ten paces.

She nodded, not trusting herself to speak. Who knew what might come out of her mouth?

Not until she reached the safety of her room, did she burst into noisy tears. He had proposed to her, and she had almost refused him? Really, she was barking mad and ought not to be allowed out of the house without a keeper.

What would Mrs. Bettina say, or Lenora? They liked Dr. Hyde and would be horrified to think she had just been trifling with his affections.

She was mad to secretly think about waiting to see if the captain survived the war. Even if he were to present himself at her door tomorrow with a bunch of flowers in his hand and beg her to marry him, she would refuse. She knew practically nothing about him. She would never marry a man she did not know to be good and honorable. He might turn out to be an arrant scoundrel, and then where would she be? All she knew about the captain was that he wrote to her in warmer terms than any man ought to write to a woman who was not his wife.

And that his words made her feel warm and loved, as Dr. Hyde's presence did not.

She threw herself full length onto the bed and wept harder than ever. Her obsession with the captain had to stop. Now, before she ruined the reality that lay in front of her. The captain was a fantasy, a figure her imagination had created out of his letters.

She did not know who he was. Not really.

If she were to meet him, she probably wouldn't even like him, let alone want to touch him as intimately as she had imagined touching him. Or allow him to take such liberties as he had so warmly described.

Really, to write such words to her, he had to be a libertine. He probably spent half his waking hours writing naughty words to women just for fun, without meaning a single word of any of them. He might seem exciting to her bored spirit, but it would not end well. He would be a drunkard and a liar, or possess a mean spirit, or be vicious.

Dr. Hyde was a good man, an honest man. He would be kind to her.

She clenched her hands into fists and pummeled the bolster on her bed with vigor. She would not wait another week to give Dr. Hyde the answer he ought to have had today. Tomorrow she would accept his offer and speak the words that would bind her to him forever as his wife.

The captain would be forgotten.

Seven

Captain Carterton rapped sharply with the head of his cane on the modest-looking door. Standing there on the street, waiting for his knock to be answered, his stomach jumped and lurched as though he'd swallowed a couple of live scorpions.

It was late to be paying a call, but he had not been able to wait until the next morning. He'd lingered at the barracks only long enough to wash, shave, and change into a fresh uniform before setting off in search of his Beatrice.

This was the moment that had kept him going through the long, lonely nights in South Africa. The moment when he would take Beatrice in his arms and claim her as his own.

The door opened and a young maidservant popped her head out into the street. All he could see was a mob cap and a pair of huge brown eyes in a pale face. "I have come to call upon Miss Beatrice Clemens." He was proud of the fact that his voice didn't shake as he spoke the name of the angel who would soon be his wife.

A faint wash of color stained her pale cheeks as she took in his freshly washed and starched uniform. "Right away, sir." She ushered him into a tiny parlor just off the front hallway and gave him a little bob as she backed into the hallway. "I'll get Miss Beatrice for you directly."

He could not sit down. He could not even stand still. Three paces to the end of the room and then three paces back again. Would she never get here?

The room was too small to hold him and all the love he carried with him. There was no space left for any air to breathe. He was on the verge of running up the stairs to go look for her himself, when the door opened and into the room walked Beatrice Clemens.

Straight into his life and into his heart.

His breath caught in his throat and his heart raced in his chest as though a thousand heavily armed Boers were chasing it across the veld. Needles of sweat prickled his forehead, tingling as if her presence burned him.

He took an involuntary step toward her, pulled irresistibly closer into her sphere. She was more beautiful in the flesh than he had imagined, even after seeing her photograph. He could hardly believe that all this feminine perfection could be his.

"Beatrice, my love." He held out his arms to her, willing her to run into them as he had dreamed for so many lonely nights. "Thank heavens we are together at last."

★ ★ ★

Temptation

Beatrice stopped dead just inside the room and stared in horror at the man standing in front of her, his arms open as if he would embrace her. This wasn't Teddy, finally come back from South Africa and here to pay her a visit as she had been expecting, but someone else entirely. Someone who seemed to have quite the wrong idea about her. The smile of welcome for her brother froze half-formed on her face. "And who may you be?" she asked, in a voice that could have made the Thames ice over.

A cloud passed over the man's face. "Beatrice? Don't you know me?" He sounded hurt and confused, like a toddler who had fallen over and scraped his knee and doesn't know why it hurts.

"Should I?" His utter certainty that she ought to recognize him threw her. She was certain she would remember meeting a man like he was. Though she was tall for a woman, this man topped her by a good four or five inches. Her muscles might be well-defined from the heavy lifting she had to do on the ward, but this man's shoulders were so broad and strong he looked as if he had spent his youth laboring on a farm. His clothes, though, showed him to be no farmer, but a gentleman.

"I am Percy. Percy Carterton." He stepped forward and took her hands in one of his. "My regiment has just returned from South Africa, and I came straightaway to ask you to be my wife."

Her stomach turned a baker's dozen somersaults in quick succession and her legs buckled with the shock. If he hadn't been holding tightly on to her, she would've stumbled and fallen.

Percy Carterton? Captain Percival Carterton? The man she

had been writing to was no longer safely far away in South Africa but back in England? In London? Standing in Mrs. Bettina's front parlor? Her head was swimming and she felt faint.

Pulling away from him, she sank down onto the closest sofa. Her mind was whirling so fast she could not think straight. She had thought he was nothing more than a fantasy on paper. Now that he was standing in front of her, whatever was she going to do with him?

"Captain Carterton," she said weakly, when her throat had unblocked enough for her to speak. "I did not expect to see you back in England." *I did not expect ever to see you*, she added silently. *I thought you were sure to tire of writing to me long before your regiment was sent home. I was so sure you were merely amusing yourself with our saucy letters, that you did not mean a single word of them.*

"I would've written to you, darling, to let you know that I was coming home, but I could not." He gestured with his chin at his right arm, and for the first time Beatrice noticed that it was in a sling of the same color as his regimental jacket.

She blinked twice in quick succession. "You were wounded?"

"Shot in the arm."

The regiment had seen real action, then. Teddy's occasional letters had been full of his desire to go into battle with the Boers or the Zulus—he didn't care which as long as he saw enough action to justify his presence in South Africa. It was strange that Teddy would be in England but had not accompanied his friend.

Assuming of course that Teddy was in England . . .

A sudden thought made a wave of true terror shudder through her. Her chest constricted so that she could not breathe, and her palms broke out into a sweat. Had he been sent to her to break the bad news of her brother? She was the only family he had left living in London. "And T . . . Teddy?" She could hardly speak past the blockage in her throat. "He was in the same regiment as you? Was he . . . ? Is he . . . ?"

"Alive and kicking," the captain said cheerfully. "He came through the bloodiest battle of the war without a scratch on him. He's joined another regiment now, and is posted safely in Pretoria. He asked me to tell you that he is well and misses you all."

The ball of lead that had been her heart lightened again at his words. "Then you have not come to give me bad news?" Her face relaxed from a rictus of fear into a trembling smile.

"Bad news? No, I am no bearer of evil tidings. I would have stepped in front of a bullet myself rather than bring you news of your brother's death." He sank to one knee in front of her, and picked up her hand in his once again. "I have come, my darling Beatrice, to ask you to be my wife."

Beatrice gaped openmouthed at him. He could not be serious. It was simply not possible. Men did not ask complete strangers to marry them. Not if they were in their right minds.

Perhaps he was a little touched in the head. During her time at St. Thomas's, she had come across old soldiers who had served in the Crimean War who had never mentally recovered from their traumatic experiences, even when their bodies were fit and well. Reality had proved to be too harsh for them—and they lived in a world of their own making.

She tugged her hand out of his and placed it firmly on her lap again. "But I have only just this minute met you. We do not even know each other," she said in her best calm nurse voice. Of all the myriad of reasons she could have chosen to show him what a mistake he was making, she could only think of this one.

He did not rise immediately from his knees. "Your letters gave me a window into your heart, a view into your soul. You showed me Beatrice as she really was, an angel of mercy, bringing light and hope to a soldier's wounded soul." His voice was deep and low, and as intense as if his whole life was riding on convincing her of his sincerity. "Ever since I received your first missive, I have dreamed of making you my wife."

"They were just letters," she protested, growing more uncomfortable with every moment that passed. Though he was living in a different reality to her own, maybe he was not touched after all. It was all the fault of those pesky letters.

Deep in her conscience she'd known that no good could come of her saucy letters, but they had been so amusing both to write and to receive. Captain Carterton's words had made her dull days lighter. She had looked forward to receiving each one as a window into another life—a life that was a lot more exciting than hers.

And if she were to be honest with herself, she had enjoyed the naughty tingle that his heated words gave her. His letters stirred her blood more than Dr. Hyde's dry touch ever had.

Many was the night she had gone to sleep dreaming of the touch of his lips on hers, or the feel of his hand on her breasts.

But it had all been a dream, a fantasy, an idle amusement to lighten her days. Nothing that was real or true. She had had no idea that the captain was writing in all seriousness, or that he fancied himself in love with her. The very notion was absurd.

The captain rose to his feet, and started to pace about the room. He filled the tiny parlor to overflowing. It was too small to hold a man his size. He towered over the small overstuffed armchairs, the lace doilies on the sideboard, and the trinkets on the mantelpiece. He did not belong in such a feminine, dainty room. "I fell in love with you when you first wrote to me. Nothing you have said or done ever since has made me change my opinion of you."

"I am sorry to hear it," she said primly, averting her eyes from him. She could not let him labor under his delusion any longer. "But I am sure you will get over your passing fancy for me. I am about to be married."

A smile, soul-deep, settled on his face. "Yes, to me."

She hated having to be the one to take that look of utter happiness away from him. "No, to a Dr. Hyde. A good man, who works in the same hospital as I do. He asked me to marry him just this afternoon, and I intend to accept him."

He stopped his pacing in midstride and simply looked at her, as if he could look into her heart and read what was written there.

In the moments of silence that followed, Beatrice could

hear the clock in the corner ticking with preternatural loudness. It deafened her. Desperately she fought the temptation to clap her hands over her ears to block out the noise of the tick-tock. The captain would think she was mad as well as cruel and capricious.

Finally he spoke. "Then you have not already given him your promise?"

"I will do so in the morning." There was no point telling him a lie. Her letters had given him too many half-truths and insinuations already, and look where her falsehoods had led her. She had made her decision to marry Dr. Hyde for the best of reasons, and everyone would have to live with it.

To her surprise, he merely shook his head with the utmost confidence, and sat down next to her on the sofa, crowding her skirts quite unnecessarily with his large frame. "You cannot love him. If you had loved him, you would've accepted him right away. If you had truly intended to marry him, you would never have written such words to me."

She bristled at his inference that she did not know her own mind. A rational and well-educated woman, she was perfectly well equipped to come to a sensible decision on such matters. "I respect and admire him. That is all I expect of a husband."

"Not love?" He shook his head slowly back and forth as if her words pained him. "That is niggardly of you. You are only giving him a half-measure, less than he has a right to expect. I feel sorry for him."

Beatrice laced her fingers together, perturbed at his nearness. It was almost as if the captain could see into the most secret corners of her heart. He was voicing the fears and doubts that she did not want to acknowledge even to herself, and making her face what she did not want to face. "He is a worthy man. In time I will grow to love him as he deserves."

"You seem very sure of such an uncertain future."

She hated the way he made her feel, as if she were doing something wrong. Marrying Dr. Hyde was the sensible choice. She knew it was. If he were in her situation, he would do exactly the same. "There is no reason why I should not become fond of him."

"And yet you have known him for how long already and your heart is still untouched? A month? Two?"

"Fourteen months, if you must know. Not that it makes any difference to my decision."

The smile on the captain's face had grown wider with every word she spoke, until it almost split his face in two. "And he has not been able to make you fall in love with him for all this time? Either he has been a sluggard in wooing you, or your heart is made of stone to resist him."

Her fingers itched to slap the look of satisfaction off his face. Just because she was not in love with her fiancé—yet—didn't mean she would break it off with him. Or, God forbid, agree to marry the captain in his place. "Love cannot be commanded."

"No, but it can be coaxed and persuaded into existence." He put his unhurt arm around her shoulders and drew her close to him. "Has he tried to coax and persuade you as I would have done? As I wrote to you in my letters?"

He felt far too good, close to her as he was. It reminded her of all the naughty words he had written to her, and made her wonder if the reality would be as good as her imagination had painted it to be.

His body gave out a male heat all of its own that made her feel as if she were sitting by a roaring fire. She wanted to curl up into him and bask in his warmth, to unbutton his shirt and slide her hands underneath his linen to stroke his warm skin. She wanted to lean into him and kiss him, taste him.

A bad idea for a woman who was determined on becoming engaged to another man in the morning.

"Dr. Hyde is a respectable gentleman. He does not need to coax or persuade me." She said the words as if they sullied her tongue just in speaking them.

A twinkle of laughter came into his eyes. He had such pretty eyes, green with a hint of tawny brown around the edges. "Every woman needs to be coaxed."

. She turned her head away from him, away from temptation. Listening to him was bad for her, just like eating too many slices of rich plum cake in one sitting was bad for her. It made her sick to the stomach, and she regretted it the moment she had licked the last delicious crumb from her lips. "I am not every woman."

"Indeed, you are not." His breath was hot on her neck, and it sent sharp red spikes of pleasure darting into her flesh. "You are Beatrice, the woman I love. The only woman in the world for me."

If she thought that eating too much plum cake was hard to resist, the temptation that the captain posed was a hundred times greater. No, a thousand times. "You do not know who I am."

"Then give me a chance, my love." His eyes were serious, pleading. His fingertips touched her cheek, lightly, reverently. It was the brush of a butterfly wing, the touch of gossamer, and it shattered her resolve into tiny shards. She would die to be touched like this. "Let me get to know you. Get to know me in return."

"And Dr. Hyde? What of him?" She crossed her arms over her chest to protect herself, to hold herself together. The touch of her bodice grated against her suddenly sensitive nipples, and she let out a tiny moan. It was too much for her. She could not fight on all fronts.

"You are not promised." His voice was demanding, inexorable.

"Not yet." It was a cry for help, a cry for mercy. If she gave in to him now, she was lost.

He had no mercy. "Do not give him your promise." His words were both a demand and a promise.

Nothing she had said or done in the last year would have given Dr. Hyde any indication she would not accept his suit. She had always intended to do so. She still intended to do so. "I must." She could not honorably refuse him. Not now. Not even though her body was crying out for the touch of the captain's hands. Dr. Hyde's courtship, and her tacit acceptance of it, had gone too far.

"Delay it, then. For a fortnight. That is all I ask."

"A week, then." She dusted her hands off and pushed him away, getting to her feet to dismiss him before she did something she would regret, like pulling up her skirts and begging him to touch her between her legs where she ached for him. So much would she give the captain, but no more. This was her life he was playing with. "Next Sunday, I shall promise Dr. Hyde that I will become his wife."

He leaned back on the sofa, his good arm behind his head, just watching her. "Unless I can convince you otherwise during that time." Despite the lateness of the hour, he was in no hurry to leave.

She walked away from him toward the window, and pulled back the curtain to look out at the night. The lamplighter had lit the streetlight on the corner, and its pale glow cast a circle of illumination at its feet.

It was easier to think straight when the captain's scent couldn't distract her, when his closeness did not make her breath catch in her throat. Her whole body still burned for him, but her desire was under her control once again.

She stared at the pale circle of light in the night. "I made up my mind a long time ago that I would marry Dr. Hyde, and I generally get what I want. He is a sensible, rational choice for a woman in my position. I have to be honest with you—for all that you wear a handsome jacket and talk prettily to me, I do not like your chances of changing my mind."

She had not heard him get up, but there he was behind her. "I always get what I want, too," he breathed into her ear. "And I want you." His lips touched the bare skin of her neck in a gentle kiss.

Then he was gone, and her neck was burning from the touch of his mouth. She put her hand to her neck, almost expecting to find it burned and blistered.

Her skin was unblemished, unmarred. But though the iron of his kiss had not marked her skin, it had branded her soul.

Captain Carterton strode down the road back to the barracks. Even at this hour, the streets were busy with all kinds of traffic: farmers coming in from the countryside with their produce to sell at the morning markets, gentlemen in top hats and canes striding home after an evening at the club, and women. Everywhere he looked there were women.

A pair of pretty girls, their skirts picked up high enough out of the mud that he could see their ankles, passed him by. He could not help smiling at them.

"Were you wanting a bit of company, then?" the bolder one of the two asked him, with a saucy wink. "A handsome gentleman like you could have the pair of us for half a crown apiece."

He gave his head a rueful shake. "Not tonight, darling." Though he was wound as tight as a watch spring, he had no interest in the myriad of pretty women that London had to offer.

Only one of them would do for him. Compared to Beatrice, no other woman was worth stretching out a hand to pluck.

"It's you as will be missing out on a grand offer, then," she retorted without any heat in her words, and the girls walked on with their heads together, giggling.

He wasn't interested in any woman's grand offer. No woman but Beatrice could tempt him.

Knowing that she had been playing him all along should have made him angry with her, but it didn't. He couldn't be angry with the woman he loved. It simply made him all the more determined to win her for himself. No paltry fool of a doctor would snatch the prize he coveted from under his nose.

She might think that she was going to wed her eligible suitor, but he knew better. No woman could respond to him as she had done if she seriously meant to marry another man. Though he had barely touched her, she had almost gone up in flames at the merest brush of his lips against her neck. Shivering, flushing—every move she made showed him how susceptible to him she was.

If she thought she could live happily with her doctor, she was fooling herself. She desired him in person as much as she had pretended to desire him in her letters. The door was wide open for him to waltz in and win her heart. He awoke the passion in her soul as her doctor so clearly did not.

She had already shown herself susceptible to his kisses. The merest touch of his lips against her skin had her jumping like a startled rabbit. The deep flush on her neck and the heaving of her chest when he came near her had merely confirmed his suspicions. She was hot for him.

Despite the naughty letters she had written to him, she was still clearly an innocent—far more innocent than he had expected her to be. Such a combination as he had found in her, a heady mix of innocence and passion, would make her an easy target for seduction.

Her doctor could not be much of a man if he had courted her for over a year and had not already kissed her senseless. Beatrice did not act like a woman who was used to being kissed senseless. Her wildness was too deeply buried—he would have to coax it out of her little by little.

Before she knew what was happening, he would have her in his arms, kissing her as she ought to be kissed.

From there, it was but a short step to having her skirts up above her waist and be dabbling his fingers in her pussy. He would be fucking her with his fingers, and she would be panting in his arms, begging for more.

He wouldn't let her come, though, not until she let him replace his fingers with his cock. Then, when she was impaled on his length, he would stroke her into pleasure.

Once he had charmed her into his bed, it would be child's play to convince her that she had to wed him. He would take her first to his bed, and then to the altar as his wife.

Traditionally, the order was reversed, but he didn't have the luxury of time. He had to win her before she settled on the doctor as the booby prize.

★ ★ ★

The following afternoon, Captain Carterton pulled up a chair and sat down next to Sergeant-Major Tofts, who was fidgeting in the hospital bed. "How's your leg doing?" The sergeant-major's leg had not healed properly since it had taken a bullet in the battle. In desperation Captain Carterton had arranged that very morning for him to be admitted to London's best hospital in a bid to save it rather than allow his friend to take the army surgeon's advice and have it amputated.

The fact that his Beatrice was a nurse at the same hospital was a delightful bonus. He could visit his friend and pay court to his beloved at the same time. She had given him a week to win her, and win her he would.

He'd stationed himself so he could see who was passing through the corridors as he sat with the sergeant-major. He'd ascertained from one of the other nurses that Beatrice was on duty in the ward today, and he would be sure to find some excuse to have her wait on his friend. With only a week to win her, he had no time to waste.

"I'm not used to staying still," Sergeant-Major Tofts admitted, as he shifted uneasily on the bed. "My backside itches from lying on it."

The captain grinned at his friend. "Just don't ask me to itch it for you. Friendship has its limits."

The doctors at St. Thomas's Hospital had cleaned out the festering wound on the sergeant-major's thigh and reset and resplinted his leg. As far as the captain could tell, they had done a decent enough job of it. Better than the army butchers who called themselves surgeons. All that remained was to see if this time it would heal well enough for him to walk again.

Despite the gray pallor of his face, the major gave him a hearty smile that showed he was not dwelling on the very real possibility that he would lose his leg. "If I'm going to be laid up anywhere, it might as well be in the hospital that boasts the prettiest nurses in London."

"They are treating you well, then?" Captain Carterton hoped so. He'd personally paid for the sergeant-major to have a private room rather than sharing a ward with a dozen other patients, thinking that the peace and quiet would aid in his friend's recovery.

"The doctors say there's a good chance of saving the leg. That's better than I expected, and as much as I can hope for." He sounded cheerfully resigned to whatever fate held in store for him.

Just then Captain Carterton caught of glimpse of a white uniform pass by. He could tell by the sway of her hips and the color of the hair underneath the white cap that it was Beatrice. He leaped to his feet and called down the corridor. "Nurse, nurse." His bass-drum boom of his voice carried through the ward.

She turned toward him at his call. A look of pleasure flickered quickly over her face before being deliberately replaced with an expression of indifference. "Yes?"

"There's a patient here who needs your help."

She hurried toward him them, her soft-soled shoes making no sound on the linoleum floor. Brushing past him, she entered the room where the sergeant-major lay. "What is the matter?" she asked, her brow creased with worry.

Captain Carterton signaled frantically to the sergeant-major behind Beatrice's back. "Invent something," he mouthed silently, willing his friend to read his meaning. "Keep her here."

"My leg . . . my leg pains me," the sergeant-major said slowly.

Captain Carterton gave a sigh of relief and smiled encouragingly at his friend.

Beatrice drew back the covers on the bed on one side and looked at the sergeant-major's bandaged leg. It had been washed and redressed earlier that morning, and the bandages looked clean and fresh. She probed at the edge of the bandages with deft fingers. "There's no evidence of swelling or infection," she murmured. "But you might be more comfortable if I elevated it a little. Let me go find you another bolster to prop it up on."

The captain watched as she walked out of the room again, her hips swaying enticingly under her gown.

"I gather that is your Miss Clemens?" the sergeant-major asked wryly, as soon as she had left. "Teddy's sister? She's a pretty young thing. Kind, too."

Carterton was still staring after her. "I'm going to marry her, you know. I'm not going to let her get away from me."

The sergeant-major heaved a sigh of envy mixed with resignation. "It's been years since I felt that way about a woman. I don't know if I have it in me anymore."

"She is my soul mate. The only woman I have ever loved." His words were no exaggeration, but the pure and simple truth. He could not imagine his life without her.

"I wondered why you were being so attentive to your old friend," the sergeant-major said with a grimace. "It's the lure of a pretty nurse, not the pleasure of my conversation, that brought you in here so bright and early this morning to see to my welfare."

The captain punched him lightly on the shoulder. "Be a good chap and find another errand for her to run for you when she comes back. One that will keep her here for a while longer."

"Can't you get your own woman? You expect your wounded comrade to play the pimp for you?"

The captain was still glaring at him when Beatrice came back in, a small, stuffed bolster in her hand. She placed it carefully under the sergeant-major's leg. "There, that should take some of the pressure off. Now, is there anything else you need to make you more comfortable?"

The sergeant-major winked at Captain Carterton behind her back. "I . . . I'd like a glass of water, please, nurse, if you're not too busy. I've got a thirst on me like a desert."

Beatrice shot a suspicious glance at the captain, but when she turned back to her patient, her face was all sweetness and light again. "Of course. I will be right with you."

When she was in the doorway, she beckoned to the captain. "Can I please have a word with you, sir, if you don't mind?"

When he followed her with alacrity, she pulled him into the empty room next door and shook her finger at him. "Don't think I don't know what you're doing."

He put on his best innocent expression. "What do you mean? Is there something wrong with keeping a wounded comrade company?"

"I am a busy woman, with other patients to look after besides your friend. I have no time to be summoned for spurious errands all day long."

"Would I do such a thing?"

She looked at him, her eyebrows raised and her arms crossed over her chest, and said nothing.

"Well, maybe I would," he admitted, "but doesn't the sergeant-major deserve to be looked after properly? He is paying for a private room. He should be able to call a nurse when he wants a drink of water, or if he just wants someone to sit with him and talk to him."

"He has you to sit and talk to him." She turned her back on him and made as if to walk out the door. "Now let me fetch him a glass of water and leave me be."

She was not getting away that easily, before he had stolen even a single kiss. He pulled her backward into his arms, and touched her cheek gently with the tip of his finger. "But I am not a pretty nurse, with red rosy cheeks." His finger crept down her neck. "Or a soft, white neck. Or breasts that are pop-

ping out of my uniform, breasts that scream to be fondled."
He suited his actions to his words, cupping her breasts in both
hands and squeezing them gently.

She gave a little squeak of surprise when he put his hands on
her. "Captain Carterton."

His cock was already hardening in his trousers at this closeness to her. He drew her firmly against him, until his hardness
was pressed up against her. He didn't want to frighten her, just
to let her see how much she affected him.

She wriggled in his arms, as if she would get away, but it
only had the effect of making him thicker and harder against
her. "You should not be doing this. Not here." Her voice came
out all breathy, and she followed up her words with a soft moan.
Her wriggling was no longer aimed at freeing herself, but at
getting closer to him.

His hands were busy at her bodice, unbuttoning her so he
could slip his hands under her clothes. "Then where should we
go? Back to your boardinghouse?"

"We should not be doing this anywhere," she sighed, press-
ing herself up against his hardness, and slipping her chemise
over her shoulders to free her breasts into his welcoming hands.
"You should not be touching me. You should not be fondling
my naked breasts."

If he'd thought he was hard before, it was nothing to how
he felt now. His cock was so stiff and swollen with desire, the
press of Beatrice's backside against him was almost painful in
its intensity.

He'd fallen in love with her mind through the letters they had exchanged, but now that he had met her he was fast falling in lust with her body. All last night he had lain awake thinking of how he would like to strip off her clothes and make love to her.

Her nipples had gone as hard as little rocks, and her breasts were heavy in his hands. His cock ached even harder as he thought about stretching her virgin cunt as he pushed into her. He wanted to bury himself inside her, lose himself inside her. "Beatrice, my love," he murmured into her ear. "How did I ever live before I met you?"

There was a narrow cot in the room, with a bare mattress on it. He sat back onto it, and pulled her down beside him. "Kiss me, Beatrice." He needed her to give him something, to touch him first.

A hesitant look came into her eyes. "I should not." But she arched her back so her breasts were pressed further into his hands.

"You want to. I can read your desire in your eyes. Why not give in to your wants, just this once? No one will ever know."

His coaxing worked. She reached toward him and gave him a tiny peck on the cheek.

With one hand on the nape of her neck, he turned her head toward him so that he could claim her mouth with his own. The first move had come from her, but the next was up to him.

Her mouth opened, and he slipped his tongue inside. She kissed him back with a passion that matched his, showing him how empty her words of denial were.

He needed to feel that she was as hot for him as he was for her. After dreaming about her for so many months, he had to feel her pussy, to taste just a little of its sweetness.

With eager hands, he pushed her skirts up to her knees and slid his hand under them. The skin of her thighs was soft and smooth, but he did not linger there. Relentlessly he pushed on until he found the slit in her drawers.

The hair on her pussy was soft and fine. He ran his fingers through her springy curls, capturing her moan of pleasure with his mouth. Carefully he parted her curls to find the treasure within, the folds that hid her cunt. He slid his hand over them, his fingers sliding slickly in the wetness. She could not deny the evidence of her body. She was hot for his cock, to have him thrust inside her. She was greedy to taste the pleasure that a man could give her. "Let me make love to you," he whispered, as he caressed her. "Let me go where no man has gone before me."

His words had the opposite effect of what he had desired. Instead of melting even further into his embrace, she pushed him away violently and scrambled back on to her feet.

He could only watch helplessly as with shaking fingers she rebuttoned her bodice. "I think you had better leave now." She would not look him in the eye as she spoke.

He was too busy trying to regain control of his rampant lust to take in what she was saying. "Beatrice, what is wrong?" He held out his arms to her, willing her back into his embrace.

"*You* are what is wrong. This whole situation is what is wrong." She wiped an angry tear from her eye as if its mere presence was a betrayal. "You took me by surprise, before I had time to steel myself against you. I am not myself when I am around you. I do not know what happens to me, but all my good sense deserts me."

"There is passion between us, Beatrice. That is nothing to be ashamed of."

His words did not mollify her, and when he came to put his arms around her, she shrugged him off like an annoying insect. "What if Dr. Hyde were to come in and find me cavorting on the bed in an empty room, like a common doxy?" she said, her voice full of angry accusation. "What then? What would I do?"

"Then you would have to marry me." It was exactly what he was aiming for after all.

He had kissed her only because he couldn't resist it, but he was sorry now that they hadn't been disturbed. Their discovery might have shortened his courtship considerably. He imagined there was nothing like being caught with a man's fingers dabbling in your pussy to make a woman suddenly amenable to marriage.

"I will be getting married to Dr. Hyde. I suggest you reconcile yourself to the fact and leave me be." She patted down her hair, tucking away a few tendrils that had worked loose. "And no more spurious errands for your friend, if you please."

He wanted to kick himself. He had pushed her too far, too fast, and now she would be doubly cautious around him. "Sergeant-Major Tofts has given everything for his country. He deserves to be waited on."

She stopped still for a heartbeat. "What did you say his name was?"

"Sergeant-Major Bartholomew Tofts."

"Was he in the same regiment as you and Teddy?" Her voice was striving to sound casual, but he could hear the keen interest shining through. Maybe Teddy had mentioned the sergeant-major in one of his letters to his sister. He was sure *he* never had. His letters had been preoccupied with more interesting matters entirely.

"We served together for a couple of years in the Transvaal. He was wounded in our last battle. The same that injured my arm."

If he were not mistaking matters, a gleam of an idea had come into Beatrice's eye at the mention of his friend's name. "If you are concerned that the sergeant-major receive the best care possible, then I suggest you hire him a private nurse." Her voice was suspiciously casual. She was planning something, he was sure of it.

Still, the idea had merit, for Sergeant-major Tofts's sake, even if not for his own. He would find other ways of coaxing Beatrice into meeting with him. "Can you recommend anyone in particular?"

"The matron of our boardinghouse is a trained nurse. She doesn't work at the hospital anymore—she hasn't since she married—but she still nurses the occasional private patient. She would be glad of the extra money." She hesitated for a moment before adding. "I think your sergeant-major and Mrs. Bettina would find they have a lot in common."

Eight

Beatrice looked at the line of people waiting to be treated. Some days, when there was sickness in the City, it snaked out the door and into the corridor, but today it was blessedly short.

At the head of the line was a very familiar face.

She gave a sigh, not sure whether it was born of irritation or of pleasure. Would Captain Carterton never let her be?

She beckoned him over with a frown. "You are not needed at the barracks?" Her voice was as stern as she could make it. She had to make him realize that she was not a pushover. He could not simply command her attention whenever he felt like it.

There might be passion between them—his kiss had taught her that much—but passion was not to be trusted. She wanted more from a husband, _needed_ more from a husband, than a good time between the sheets.

A husband was forever. A woman had to choose wisely when she picked the man she would marry, and not allow herself to be blinded by transient bodily desires. She did not know the captain's character, and she certainly doubted the permanence of his affections. In fact, she suspected he was poor husband material all around.

If she was a different sort of woman, she might consider taking him as a temporary lover. He would do very well for that sort of thing. Just the thought of him lying over her, pushing his cock into her secret places, was enough to make her squirm with heat.

Unfortunately she was not in the market for a lover . . .

The captain gestured at his wounded arm, seemingly not at all concerned by the sternness of her voice. "I'm officially on invalid leave. A soldier, even an officer, isn't much good if he's only got one arm. I've come to have the dressings changed."

"Could the army surgeons not oblige you?" In her experience, the army surgeons were jealous of their patients and only sent the most intractable cases to the public hospital.

He gave her a cheeky grin. "They are not as pretty as you are."

"If you have come to see me in my professional capacity, I trust you will keep the conversation appropriate," she said in her most quelling tone.

"I waited for you. I wanted it to be your hands that healed me, not the hands of a stranger."

"The result would be the same."

His smile crinkled the corner of his eyes. "Ah, but the process would be so much less pleasant."

She gave a sigh. Mules had nothing on his stubbornness. She might as well give in to him graciously and save her energy for the battles that really mattered. Like resisting his physical appeal. "Let me take off your sling and see what's underneath."

He held out his arm to her. She untied the sling and carefully unwound the bandages the covered his arm.

She recoiled at the sight of the nasty red gashes that covered his upper arm. The red lines sprawled out over his arm like the tracks of a wandering centipede. She tried not to let the shock show on her face at the sight, but she could not help letting a gasp of indrawn breath escape her. "A bullet did all this to you?" It looked as if his arm had been put in a mangle and the handle turned until his arm was nothing but a bloody pulp.

"The bullet did part of it. The rest was done by a surgeon digging out the bullet and all the pieces of bone it shattered."

"I hope he was a good surgeon," she muttered, as she tested the edges of each cut.

He held himself stock-still, not twitching so much as a single muscle on his face, as she probed at his cuts. "An army surgeon. He'd had plenty of practice stitching up bullet wounds."

The whole arm was a mass of yellow and green from fading bruises. The cuts appeared to be healing well, with no sign of infection. "Can you move it?"

He gave it an exploratory swing. "I'm not sure my shoulder joint will ever be the same again," he said, a grimace of pain flitting over his face. "And I doubt I'll be much good with a spade. But it should work well enough for my purposes—to raise a standard, ride a horse, fire a rifle. It won't get me invalided out of the army permanently. That's all I care about."

"So you'll still be Captain Carterton."

"I will always be Captain Carterton," he replied proudly. "Once a captain, always a captain."

"Just as I shall always be a nurse, I suppose." She fetched a pot of ointment from a cupboard and smoothed it carefully over his arm. "The cuts are healing nicely, but soon they'll start to itch, if they don't already. Don't scratch them—it will impede their healing and may cause them to get inflamed or infected. I will give you a bottle of ointment to take away with you. Rub it into your arm every day and it should stop the skin from getting too uncomfortably dry and scaly."

He looked askance at the pot of ointment and made no move to take it from her. "Isn't that what you nurses are for? To tend to your patients' wounds?"

"Nurses are here to do what their patients cannot do for themselves. Not what they are simply too lazy to do for themselves," she scolded him. She didn't need to give him another excuse to follow her around and invent tasks for her to do under the guise of needing assistance.

"You could see to my arm every day. It would not take you long. And then you would be sure that the ointment was applied in accordance with your high standards, and not just slapped on willy-nilly by a careless soldier in a hurry to visit his sweetheart."

His skin under her hands was warm, not with the heat of fever but with the warmth of life. She could happily smooth ointment into his skin for an hour on end. "You are the one who will suffer if you forget." Just being this close to him was a treat for her foolish senses.

Everything about him was so tempting. The softness of his skin, the knowledge that he had been wounded in the service of his country, even the curl of his moustaches all made her want to take him in her arms and press him close to her heart.

It was a foolish reaction for an almost engaged woman to have to a man who was not her almost-fiancé. Unfortunately, she could not always control her desire with the force of her common sense.

He was looking at her with big puppy-dog eyes, begging her to take pity on him. "And you became a nurse to reduce the suffering in the world."

She shook her head mournfully at him. He was clearly determined to get his own way. She may as well just give in gracefully. "Come and see me early in the mornings, before my shift starts, and I will spend a couple of minutes attending to you."

A smile like a beam of sunshine on a winter's day brightened his face. "I knew you had a generous heart."

She put the ointment away and fetched some clean bandages, which she wound carefully around his injured arm. Allowing the gashes to remain covered would keep them clean and promote their healing. "But only five minutes. No more. And you must behave yourself or I will refuse to see you again."

"With a threat like that, I will be on my best behavior." He leaned closer to her so none of the others in the busy clinic could hear him. "I will be so well behaved that I will not even beg you for a kiss."

She stepped back and fixed him with a glare. "See that you don't. Now run away and find something else to amuse you. Go play with your toy soldiers or something. I have more patients to attend to."

"Toy soldiers?" He gave a huff of affronted pride. "Me, a wounded veteran of the Transvaal Rebellion, play with toy soldiers? You insult me."

She gave him a little push. "Off you run, there's a good little captain."

He gave an easy shrug. "If you insist. I need to give my troop of French soldiers a new coat of paint anyway. Their jackets are looking quite chipped and dirty." He brushed past her face with his own in what might have been a parting kiss, and then he was gone.

Beatrice watched him go before she turned to the line of patients waiting to see her and called the next one up. One thing was clear—she could not tell Dr. Hyde that she would marry him while her foolish attraction to Captain Carterton was raging out of control. She could not agree to marry one man while she was dreaming of making love to another—it would not be fair to either of them.

Captain Carterton had the knack of making her go weak at the knees just by looking at her. Without a single touch, he could have her panting with need for him, with desire for his hands on her body, his lips on hers. She could not see him without being reminded of the words he had written to her, the words of both desire and of love. He wanted her in the most elemental way that a man wanted a woman, and her body responded to him in kind.

She wanted him to take control of her, to take possession of her, as she had never wanted any other man. She wanted to feel him thrusting inside her, making her his woman. She wanted him to take her. To fuck her, just as he had described in his letters.

The need to touch him came back stronger every time she fought it off. She caught herself at odd moments during the day obsessing over how his hair would feel under her fingers, how smooth his chest would be, and how his member might swell and grow at her touch. She wanted to find out everything about him, and more.

Even more annoyingly, she had discovered that not only did she desire him, but she liked him. He was generous and attentive to his wounded friend, by turns charming and passionately affectionate to her, and bravely uncomplaining about his injury even though she could see that it had to be terribly painful.

He made her heart lift just to see him. She could not help liking him. That was more dangerous even than the passion she felt. Such passion as he aroused in her would be a fleeting sensation. It must be. Nothing that strong and hot could last without burning itself out.

Eventually he would tire of pursuing her, and her wayward passions would settle down from a raging inferno into a gentle simmer. She would mourn its passing, even though she knew it was for the best. He had built his affection for her on a fantasy. It would wither and die as quickly as it had sprung up.

Once that happened, she could once again think clearly and with a level head about Dr. Hyde's offer. But until then, she would have to avoid the doctor's company.

After leaving Beatrice in the hospital, Captain Carterton strode over to the boardinghouse where she lived. She had suggested the matron as a private nurse for Sergeant-Major Tofts, and he was anxious to settle the matter with her, if he could. Though the sergeant-major's leg seemed to be healing well enough, his friend did not seem to be healing as well in spirit as he was in body. A pretty nurse to attend to him and to keep him company when he had no other visitors would be just what he needed.

The matron was an attractive woman, no longer in the first flush of youth. He introduced himself and explained his errand.

"A private nurse?" She pursed her lips together. "I haven't practiced as a nurse for some years now. I'm not sure I would be up to the task."

Captain Carterton had immediately warmed to her. The few minutes he had spent in her company had already made him sure that she would be the perfect antidote to the sergeant-major's dullness of spirits. "Beatrice, Miss Clemens, said you took on the odd nursing job still. She suggested you would be perfect for the task."

"I have accepted the odd position, taking care of elderly folk, mostly," Mrs. Bettina said with a self-deprecating smile. "They need a bit of care and attention, but not serious nursing. Not like a wounded man."

"My friend is the same as any other man. He needs company and care more than anything else. And you could always call on the nurses on the wards to help you, if you needed something. I'm sure he would be very grateful for the attention. As would I."

"Could I work around the times I need to be here for my girls?" she asked him anxiously. "They are my first duty. I cannot neglect them for another position."

"That would be perfectly acceptable," he assured her. "I would not have any of them suffering because you were busy elsewhere."

"And you would want me to start quite soon?"

"The sooner the better. But I'm sure my friend can wait a few days, if that suits you better," he added hastily, as a look of concern passed over her face.

"My cook is away until Wednesday, and I am running the boardinghouse by myself," she explained. "But I could start on Thursday."

"That would be perfect." He stretched his legs out in front of him. He had achieved one of his goals for the afternoon. The other would not be quite so straightforward. "It's remarkably warm for this time of year, isn't it? I worked up quite a thirst walking over here."

Mrs. Bettina jumped to her feet. "Oh, where are my manners. I completely forgot to offer you a cup of tea. I swear, I am all at sixes and sevens with Agatha away."

"I would love a cup of tea, but please, do not put yourself out. Let me come and help you."

"No, I will have the maid bring it to us." She rang the bell, and instructed the girl who answered to bring in a pot of tea. "And make sure the water boils and put two big spoonfuls of tea into the pot," she added, for good measure.

"She is a good, hard worker, but a little slow to learn new things," she explained to the captain, as the girl ran off to do her bidding.

"I'm sure all the girls who board with you are hard workers," he said approvingly. "Miss Clemens, for example. She made a thoroughly good job of bandaging up my arm again just this morning."

A knowing look came into Mrs. Bettina's eyes. "She is a fine young woman. And very pretty, too."

"Extremely." He paused for a moment. "I would like to thank her for taking such good care of my arm, but I don't know how to. Is she a young lady who loves nature and would like a pretty bunch of violets? That seems so paltry a gift in recompense for her care. I had thought about a pair of silk stockings, but . . ." He shook his head and let his voice tail off. "They are too . . . too personal a gift. I own, I am in a quandary for an appropriate gift for her."

Mrs. Bettina was looking at him with approval. "You are a

thoughtful gentleman to put such effort into finding the right gift for her. Dr. Hyde takes her walking in the park every weekend to listen to the brass band. He is a good man, but after a year he still does not know that she does not like the park and she hates brass bands and would much rather go to a music hall." She shook her head in despair. "He does not listen."

"She likes music halls?"

"Who doesn't?" Mrs. Bettina smiled. "I've been known to go myself on the odd occasion. A nurse's salary doesn't afford many luxuries, but the girls make up a party to go the music halls once every few months."

Just then the tea arrived, and Mrs. Bettina poured him out a cup. She waited until he had taken a sip. "I am only telling you this because I am sure Dr. Hyde is not the man for Beatrice," she blurted out.

He nearly choked on his mouthful of tea. Clearly he had not been as subtle as he had thought. "I quite agree."

"She is not in love with the doctor. Not as a young woman ought to be in love with the man she marries. But what can I say to convince her there is more to life than she knows? Every woman needs to find that out for herself." She paused and took a sip of her own tea. "What's more, I do not believe that Dr. Hyde is in love with her, for all he has asked her to be his wife. That would be a marriage of convenience on both sides. Nothing more."

"I would offer her more than such an empty marriage. I would offer her love, too. And I would listen to her."

She gazed steadily at him, as if she could read his thoughts. "You would offer her marriage?" Her face went a little pink around the edges but she did not look away. "You must forgive me for asking, but she is a good girl, and is very dear to me. I would not have you hurt her in any way."

"Yes, I would offer her marriage." He shifted uncomfortably on his chair, but Mrs. Bettina deserved to be told the truth. "In fact, I already have."

"And her answer?"

He squared his shoulders. An officer in the English army did not accept defeat. "I have hopes she will accept me the next time I ask her. If not, then the time after that. Because I will not stop asking until she says yes."

"You care for her that much?"

"I do."

"Then I shall not regret telling you of her love for music halls. Or that her shift finishes early tomorrow, and she would have plenty of time to come back here to dress before heading out for the evening."

In Mrs. Bettina he had found an unexpected ally in his quest. He rose from his chair and bent over to kiss her hand. "You will not regret your confidence in me."

She rose, too, to see him to the door. "See that I don't," were her parting words as he walked out and onto the street.

Captain Carterton was waiting outside the hospital for Beatrice when her shift finished the following afternoon.

She raised her eyebrows at him as he fell into step beside

her. "Do your bandages need changing again already? Or is it something else this time? Your leg, perhaps? Or maybe there is something wrong with your head?"

She wished he wasn't quite so handsome in his civilian clothes. The elegant cut of his trousers showed off the fine trim of his leg, and his waistcoat buttoned over a broad chest and flat stomach. Not that she should be looking at his chest or his stomach. Or his legs. Or the bits in between. Definitely not those. But he was a fine figure of a man nonetheless, even when he left his red jacket back at the barracks.

Her snippy attitude just made him laugh. "There is nothing wrong with my head. But I thank you for asking."

"Then what can I do for you?"

He offered her his arm. "I have come to walk you home."

It was gallant of him, she supposed, but hardly necessary. "I am quite used to walking home by myself." His company was far more dangerous to her than anyone she could meet on the streets.

"Do you treat all your suitors in such a cavalier fashion? Tut, tut, Beatrice, that is no way to catch a man. We men like to think of you women as hothouse flowers, unable to survive without our protection."

"Then you men are fools."

"That is harsh."

"A man should understand a woman's strengths as well as her weaknesses. And he should prize her all the more for them."

"I prize you for your compassion and your forthrightness."

She unbent so far as to place her hand in the crook of his elbow. "Thank you."

"And for your skill with your hands, too. I swear my arm feels much better since you rubbed the ointment into it this morning."

"I am glad of it."

"And for your honesty."

That was slightly unexpected. "Thank you again."

"For your honesty which will compel you to admit that, yes, indeed, you would love to accompany me to the London Pavilion music hall this evening."

She stopped walking and stared at him. "You have bought tickets to the London Pavilion?" She had wanted to go and see the new music hall for weeks now, but such indulgences did not come cheaply and her salary was not extravagant.

"You work so hard, I thought you might appreciate an evening out. We can dine there while we watch the show."

"Just the two of us?" It would hardly be proper, not when she had still to give Dr. Hyde an answer to his proposal, but how she would love to go.

"You do want to go, don't you?"

"I would love to see the London Pavilion." She could not possibly pretend indifference to such an offer. If she could not be a nurse, she would love to be a singer in a music hall. What a life they had—to hold an audience in the palm of their hand as they crooned a beautiful love song, or danced their way through a sparkling comedy. It must feel almost as good as healing the sick, for they, too, healed people in their own way. They healed people by making them laugh, by taking them out of their gray lives for just a few hours and showing them fun and happiness. He had hit upon the one offer that she could not resist.

"Then it is settled. I will wait in Mrs. Bettina's parlor while you change out of your uniform, and then we can take a hansom cab to the West End."

Dr. Hyde had never taken her to a music hall, she thought rather morosely, as she stripped off her nurse's uniform and gave herself a hurried wash in a basin. He had never offered, and she would never ask him—that was not the sort of relationship they shared. If she were eventually to marry him, she might never go to a music hall again. Which made her all the more determined to enjoy the show with the captain this evening.

She riffled through her wardrobe, hastily picking out her favorite dress. Pale green silk, with more frills and ruffles than she usually wore; it had been a gift from her sister, Louisa, who had insisted on buying it for her on her last visit home. She had not worn it before—it was too good for everyday use. But for a visit to the London Pavilion, to eat a fine dinner and watch a show, it was perfect.

She dressed as quickly as she could. It felt strange to think that Captain Carterton was sitting in the parlor just downstairs while she was walking around upstairs in her underclothes. The thought made her nipples grow hard, as if she had just washed in cold water. It really didn't seem at all proper, but Mrs. Bettina hadn't seemed at all worried by the idea so it must not be too shocking.

She glanced at herself in the mirror. The dress was perfect, but she couldn't go out with her hair looking the way it did. She pulled the hairpins out of her bun and shook her hair down over her shoulders. Ah, it felt good to get the weight of it off the back of her neck for a few moments. There wasn't time to give it the fifty strokes with the brush it needed to make it shine, but no matter. She tied it up into a loose bun and repinned it carefully.

One last look in the mirror. Yes, she was ready.

Captain Carterton had hailed a hansom cab, and it was waiting outside for them. She climbed into it with a growing sense of excitement. The London Pavilion had recently been given a facelift and fitted out with marble columns in the entryway. It looked fabulous from the outside—she could only imagine what the inside would be like. And the show itself promised to be a fine one. The famous tenor Señor Fratelli himself was singing. She had wanted to hear him forever.

Captain Carterton climbed in beside her and called for the driver to be off.

The drive through the quiet streets was mercifully short. The hansom cab was too small for Beatrice to feel comfortable in, not with the captain sitting next to her with his shoulders touching hers and his legs pressed against her own from thigh to ankle. She tried to move further into the corner to put some distance between them, but there was no space to maneuver. In the end, she sat back on the seat and tried to ignore the feelings that his touch ignited deep in her stomach. She was off to see a show at the London Pavilion and nothing could put a dent in the happy bubble of her mood.

The façade of the building was as grand as anything could be. Tall columns of marble stretched up toward the sky, framing a grand entranceway that had to be three or four times her height. Captain Carterton escorted her inside, where they were seated at a table close to the stage.

"We have the best seats in the house," she sighed happily, as she gave her coat to the hovering attendant.

"Nothing but the best for my Beatrice," he murmured, pulling out the chair for her so she could sit down.

The table top was made of marble, and cool to the touch. She leaned her elbows on it and looked at the stage. It was still empty and covered with a thick red curtain, but she could sense the excitement building up behind the scenes. She could feel the same excitement buzzing in the pit of her stomach.

The attendant was back again in a moment. "What would you care for dinner?"

Beatrice could summon little interest in food. "I don't know. Whatever."

With an easy smile at her distractedness, Captain Carterton took over and ordered for both of them, checking with her that his choices were satisfactory.

She sat staring at the curtain, tapping her fingers on the table and every so often glancing to the sides of the curtain to see if she could make out any movement.

"Have patience." He got out his fob watch and showed her the time. "They will not begin for another quarter of an hour or more."

"I have never been a patient person," she confessed. "When I see something I want, I want it now. Without having to wait."

He looked meaningfully at her. "Then we are alike, you and I. For I, too, have little patience when it comes to getting what I want."

She could not mistake his meaning. It was as clear as the light from the scores of gas lamps that lit up the whole pavilion. He wanted her, and he intended to have her.

She blushed under his scrutiny, not knowing what to say. The attendant bringing out a plateful of oysters for both of them saved her from having to make any reply.

She tucked into them with gusto, wiping her fingers on her napkin. Captain Carterton must have a reasonable income stashed away to afford to take her out to dinner in a place such as this. And he was kind, too. Maybe he would not make such a bad husband after all.

She squelched that thought quickly. After witnessing her sister Emily's disastrous marriage to a man she barely knew, she had vowed never to make the same mistake. She would not marry anyone until she was quite sure they were utterly respectable, and had no dark secrets they were hiding. Falling in love with a stranger may sound appealing, but she had seen firsthand the results. No, love at first sight was not for her.

Dr. Hyde, she knew, was a good man, who would not beat his

wife or be cruel to his children. Charming companion though he was, she was a good deal less sure of the captain's temperament.

The plate littered in empty oyster shells had just been removed when a man appeared between the curtains. He swept off his hat and gave a low bow to a smattering of applause. "Ladies and gentlemen, it is my honor to present to you this evening, as the first act in our incomparable show, the esteemed, the enviable, the utterly enchanting, Miss Kitty Feathers."

Another round of applause, louder this time, as a woman dressed for all the world as a man in tails and spats, strutted on to the stage twirling a cane in her hand.

Beatrice drew a deep breath. Miss Kitty Feathers was a male impersonator. She'd never seen one before, not a good one— only a silly girl who'd wiggled her hips in a suit and looked nothing like a man at all. Miss Kitty was something else altogether. She walked just like a man, and her singing voice was deeper than a woman's usually was. If it hadn't been for the obvious femininity of her face, Beatrice would've sworn she was looking at a man on the stage.

The male impersonator was followed by a man at the piano who sang a pair of catchy ballads, and then by a troupe of dancing girls.

So intent was she on watching the show that she hardly noticed the food that was put in front of her. She ate distractedly, barely taking her eyes off the stage.

The man at the piano sang a comic song, and Captain Carterton laughed uproariously at his risqué jokes. He was enjoying himself as much as she was. She relaxed into her chair a little more, glad that he wasn't sitting there stiff and unamused, as Dr. Hyde no doubt would have been.

It was a pity Dr. Hyde was such a stuffed shirt. Going to the music hall was so much more fun than listening to a dreary brass band play horrid marching songs on a dull day in the park.

By the time Señor Fratelli came out to sing, she had laughed so hard and clapped so hard she had little more in her to give. But the music hall had one last thrill to give her. His singing was so beautiful it brought tears to her eyes.

Cutting through the enraptured applause that followed his act, came the finale for the evening—"Land of Hope and Glory." She sang along with the rest of the audience, Captain Carterton's fine baritone in her ear.

Surreptitiously she wiped the tears away from her eyes. The London Pavilion had lived up to its reputation, and given her a night to remember.

It was with a sense of regret she accepted her coat back from the attendant.

Their hansom cab was waiting for them a little way down the road as the captain had requested. She took hold of his arm, huddling close to him for protection from the biting wind that had sprung up. "Thank you for taking me to the music hall. I loved every minute of it."

"It was my pleasure. I enjoyed myself even more watching your pleasure." He sounded as though he really meant it.

Temptation

He handed her into the hansom cab and climbed in after her. The streets were dark now, with only the light of the gas lamps to show where they were going. The driver cracked the whip and set his horses off smartly.

In the darkness he moved closer to her and put one arm around her shoulder. "Captain Carterton," she protested under her breath so the driver would not hear. "That is hardly proper."

"It is dark. No one can see us. And don't I deserve a kiss for taking you to the music hall tonight?"

His breath was hot on her neck. If she were to turn her head just a little to the side, she could kiss him and find out just how good he tasted.

He brushed his fingers gently over her cheek. "Do you want me to kiss you?"

"Not at all," she lied.

"Beatrice, Beatrice. Didn't I say earlier today that your honesty was one of the things I loved most about you? And then for you to tell such a monstrous fib as that . . ." He let his voice tail off into a note of ineffable sadness.

She giggled just a little, the happiness at such a wonderful evening having gone to her head. "You are terribly sure of yourself."

She could feel his answering smile in the darkness. "I'm told it's one of my best qualities."

"But I don't really want you to kiss me. It would not be wise." She hated having to be wise all the time.

"I can understand your feelings on the matter. I know how

difficult you find it to control yourself when you are around me. I can understand you would not want to embarrass yourself."

"Do not misunderstand me." She crossed her arms over her chest defiantly. "That is not the reason at all."

"You mean you are confident you will be able to keep a lid on your passion? Even if I were to lean over and touch my lips to yours?"

"Of course I can."

"Excellent. Then I see no reason not to kiss you."

He pulled her close to him and kissed her gently. The motion of the hansom cab made judging distances difficult, and he bumped his nose against hers. "Damn cobblestones," he growled. "They were designed by old Puritans who never tried to kiss their sweethearts in a light carriage."

He solved the problem by pulling her onto his lap, where she sprawled, half sitting, half lying on top of him. "Much better," he murmured, wrapping his arms around her. "Now I can kiss you without worrying I will accidentally break your nose."

She opened her mouth to protest against the indignity of being plastered against him in the cab, and he took advantage of the opportunity to claim her lips with his own.

Laudanum—that was what he was to her good sense. One taste of him and she forgot all her principles, all her morals. She was no better than an opium addict, a poor soul who would never be cured of her cravings. A single taste of him was all it took to send desire flowing through her body so strongly she could not resist it.

She opened her mouth to his, letting him taste her. What did she care that the hansom cab driver was sitting up behind them on his seat? His eyes ought to be on the road, steering them past the hazards of the London streets, not on what his passengers were doing. And even if he could see them in the gloom, what did she care? No doubt he had seen many a worse things in his travels over the streets.

The captain was not content with plundering her mouth. His hands stroked her thighs and then tugged up her skirts until her boots and stockings were exposed.

They passed a group of revelers on the corner who hooted and catcalled at the glimpse she afforded them of her stock-inged legs through the quickly fogging window of the carriage, but the hansom quickly passed them by.

He kept on kissing her while his hands crept up her thighs, making their way unerringly to the slit in her drawers. His fingers had felt so good on her pussy when he had kissed her in the hospital that she had no will to stop him from touching her there again.

Her whole body quivered as his hands brushed over her curls. When he parted her folds and slipped one finger inside her, she thought she would faint with the pleasure.

Dr. Hyde had never touched her in this way. She couldn't imagine him fondling her in such a public place. She couldn't even imagine him fondling her like this in the privacy of their marital bedroom. A quick fumble under her nightgown, maybe. That would be all the pleasure she'd get from such a dry stick.

Just then the hansom cab pulled up outside the boarding-house where she lived. She tried to push him away and sit up, but he wouldn't let her. "Drive on," he called to the driver. "Take us to St. James's Park."

"But . . ."

He hushed her with his mouth against hers. "I haven't tasted nearly enough of you. In the quietness and seclusion of the park we can snatch a few more moments of privacy so you and I can get to know each other better."

To tell the truth, she didn't want him to take his finger out of her pussy quite yet. She would agree to anything he suggested as long as he continued to stroke her into oblivion.

The park was dark and deserted, just as Captain Carterton had hoped. The driver pulled up and let the cab come to a stop. The captain scrabbled in his pocket for a couple of guineas and handed them up to the driver. "Take yourself off for a while. I'll call you when I want you to come back."

The driver whistled between his teeth as he took the money. "Sure thing, guv," he said, as he clambered down from the box and headed off into the darkness.

The captain watched him as he wandered out of sight behind some trees.

Perfect. They were alone now, and he could get on with his task of seducing Beatrice into his arms. It was a pity he hadn't ordered a larger, hackney cab, rather than the smaller, two-wheeled hansom cab. There wasn't enough room in the hansom to fuck her properly, and the wind was too cold to make lying on the grass a very pleasant prospect.

Next time he took her out, he would order a hackney cab and then make love to her under cover while the driver took them around the streets of London.

For now, he would have to improvise.

"There, now we are all alone," he whispered. It wasn't quite true—he could see the eyes of the hansom cab driver glinting in the trees not far away. He was standing in the shadows, watching them, but Captain Carterton didn't care. The driver could watch all he wanted, but no man but he was going to touch Beatrice's body. Knowing he had an audience just made him all the more determined not to fail in getting her where he wanted her to be.

His finger was still in her pussy. She was wet, too, and getting wetter. Slowly he withdrew it a little way and then pushed back into her. "Mmmm," he murmured into her ear. "That feels so good. Do you like it, too? Do you like knowing my finger is inside you? Do you like being fucked by my finger?"

Her cunt had a virgin's tightness and he had to push hard to get his finger more deeply inside her. Her muscles clenched around him in protest at the invasion. She gasped a little as he thrust harder and wriggled her hips against him. "Yes, I like it."

He withdrew his finger all the way then, and teased the little nub at the top of her pussy. It was as hard as a pebble, and she moaned as he flicked it. "Or do you want me to stop?" He had no intention of stopping for long, but he would at least give her the illusion of choice.

She thrust herself against his finger, encouraging him to push inside her again. "No, don't stop."

He liked having her ask him to make love to her, having her beg him to put his finger into her again. He thrust his finger into her again, harder this time, forcefully pushing through the barriers her body tried to put in his way.

Her cunt was throbbing against his finger, clutching on to him. His cock, which had stayed semi-hard all evening, leaped to life at the prospect of having her intimate muscles clench around him.

Christ, he wanted to fuck her. He wanted to push her skirts aside, rip off her drawers, and thrust into her with all the finesse of a raging elephant. He wanted to fuck her until he came hard and fast in her pussy, and then he wanted to turn her over, take her from behind, and fuck her all over again. He wanted to fuck her over and over until his cock was so drained and limp that it couldn't stand up again for a week.

But that would be counterproductive. He had to get her eating out of his hand, craving his touch, wanting more and more. He needed to give her a hint of the pleasure she could find in his arms, to make her welcome his touch.

Slowly, gently, he would lead her on until allowing him to make love to her was the next inevitable step. He had already gotten her used to the feeling on his finger inside her, and she no longer quibbled when he touched her there. Little by little he would tempt her into further intimacies with him, until she hardly noticed when he replaced his finger with his mouth, his tongue, his cock.

He guided her hand to the buttons of his trousers, encouraging her to stroke his hardness through his trousers. "Touch me as I am touching you," he urged her. "Make me feel as good as you feel."

With tentative hands, she stroked him through the fabric. It wasn't enough for him. Not nearly enough. He reached down and undid the buttons and slid her hand inside his drawers.

Her hand was on his cock. It was almost enough to make him come right then and there, to spurt his hot seed into her soft hand.

He couldn't lose control so soon, not when so much was at stake.

Getting to his knees on the cab floor in front of her, he raised her skirts to the waist and undid the ties on her drawers. Then he put his head in between her legs and breathed in the essence of her.

Her hands were tangled in his hair as she tried to push him away. "What are you doing?"

"Tasting you." He bent his head and licked her pussy, right across the folds that hid her cunt, and swirling his tongue around the hard nub of her clit. She gave a scream of pleasure and the hands in his hair pulled him closer.

Out of the corner of his eye, he could see the cab driver drawing closer, until he was only a few feet away and frankly staring at them.

He pushed his finger back into her pussy as he licked her nub. His cock was standing up to attention, having forced its way out of his unbuttoned trousers. Licking her pussy was making it as hard as stone, and he could feel his balls tighten and retreat into his body. A simple touch would be enough to send him over the edge now.

The cab driver had his hand in his pants now and was stroking himself as he watched them. Captain Carterton envied his simplicity—he had no shame in spying in them and finding a release that way.

The captain licked at Beatrice desperately, urgently needing to give her satisfaction so he could find his own release. He wanted her satiated, not frustrated and unfulfilled.

With his free hand he reached down to stroke his cock. His orgasm was on the brink of exploding out of him, but he was too much of a gentleman not to let a lady go first.

Roughly now he fucked her with his finger, driving her need to breaking point. He had to get her there. He had to make her come.

Finally she gave a cry and her muscles clenched around his finger. She held herself still, and then her pussy throbbed violently around him and when he sucked on her clit, she shuddered uncontrollably.

Only just in time. With a few strokes, his own seed splattered out onto the floor of the hansom cab. Out of the corner of his eye, he could see the driver milking himself of his come, creaming over the wheel of his cab.

Her pussy was so sweet and soft. Even though he'd just orgasmed, he could not resist tasting her again. He bent his head and licked her once again, making her jump as his tongue passed over her clit.

"When you are my wife, I will feast on your pussy every night," he murmured, as he reluctantly removed his head from between her thighs and allowed her skirts to drop back to the floor of the cab. The hem dragged in his come, lying sticky on the floor. He was perversely glad to see its wetness stain her skirts. When she left the cab tonight, she would carry a little piece of him with her.

"When I am married to someone else, I will never travel anywhere in a hansom cab with you," she replied smartly. "Or in any other conveyance, for that matter."

"Dr. Hyde might not marry you if he were to see another man's head between your naked legs," he reminded her coarsely. "Men have this funny desire that their wives come to them untouched by any other man."

"I am still a virgin." Her voice was tart, though he could hear an undercurrent of worry.

"Not by much. You've had my finger inside you twice, and now my tongue. It wouldn't take much for me to get my cock inside you." He probably shouldn't give away his tactics, but her repeated assurances that she was going to marry Dr. Hyde put him out of temper. She was not going to marry anyone but him.

"But you haven't got your cock inside me yet," she replied,

her voice filled with anger. "If I had any sense, I would marry before you ruin me."

He bit back the words on the tip on his tongue. Instead, he called to the driver who, after coming on the wheel, had retreated a safe distance away from the cab to tuck himself back into his pants again. "Drive us back to Westminster, on the double."

The man doffed his hat and climbed back up onto his perch behind the cab. With a crack of his whip, the horses got underway.

The rode in silence through the dark streets. The wheels clattered over the cobblestones, grinding the cab driver's come into the dust.

Captain Carterton was still stewing over her words when they pulled up to the boardinghouse for the second time that night. As she clambered down from the cab, he held her back with a hand on her arm. "Make no mistake about it, Beatrice. The next time I get you alone, I shall have your skirts above your waist and my cock will be demanding entrance to your wet little cunt. There will be no stopping me. You will not want to stop me.

"Then, when I have fucked you well, you will have little choice but to accept me as your husband."

Nine

The next morning before her shift started, Beatrice unwound the bandages on Captain Carterton's arm. Though it looked as bad as it had the day before, it had lost its power to horrify her. It was just a wound, and one that seemed to be healing well. He was one of the lucky ones.

She fetched the jar of ointment and began to rub it into his skin, all without looking at him in the eyes. She hadn't behaved very properly toward him last night. First, by allowing him to be so familiar with her person, and then by upbraiding him for his familiarity.

Not that he deserved her politeness. Never had she met such an unrepentant rake as Captain Carterton. He was the sort of man her mother, if she had still been alive, would have warned her against.

She should never have agreed to go to the music hall with him, however much she wanted to hear Señor Fratelli sing. He had caught her at a weak moment, when her defenses were low. Now he had quite the wrong idea about her. She was not a gay girl to be fucked in the park for the price of admittance to a music hall, but a respectable young woman.

"Does your arm still hurt?" she mumbled ungraciously, as he winced under her less than tender ministrations. She wasn't *trying* to hurt him, but she wasn't trying terribly hard *not* to hurt him, either.

"Only when you yank it around like it was a rag doll," he grumbled back again.

"You could put the ointment on yourself if you don't like the way I do it." She was in the mood for a quarrel. Arguing with him was preferable to wishing he would kiss her again.

"I can't reach it properly. Besides, it hurts less when you do it."

She smoothed the ointment into his skin, trying not to think about how she had felt when his hands were touching her last night in the carriage. "That's not what you said a moment ago."

He was silent as she worked her way carefully around the worst of the gashes. "I still want to marry you, you know. Now more than ever."

So he had said the night before, but she had only half believed him. "We are in the hospital. Not an appropriate place to discuss such things." Especially not when any number of other people were clustered around the ward: doctors examining patients, nurses scurrying to and fro on errands, not to mention the patients themselves.

"Then, will you come out to another music hall with me

tonight? Maybe to the Alhambra? I hear their dancing girls are quite spectacular, not to mention rather saucy. I shall tell you again there. Or maybe during the cab ride home again."

He was no gentleman to remind her of their last cab ride together. "I will not be going to any music hall with you in the future."

"You did not enjoy yourself last night?"

She smothered her gasp of embarrassment with a cough. "The music hall was very fine."

"And the rest of the evening?"

She wound the bandages around his arm with a savage intensity. "Please, be quiet. I do not want to talk about it. Especially not here, while I am at work."

"But I do." His voice was a seductive whisper, pitched too low to carry to anyone else in the vicinity. "I want to talk about how soft your skin was, and how wet you were when I stroked your pussy. I want to tell you how delicious you tasted, and how I imagined it was my cock your cunt was squeezing as you orgasmed."

His words dripped into her ear like poison, each of them etching away at her conscience until she could not bear it. "I do not want to hear you," she hissed, winding his bandages so quickly they tangled. "Be quiet and do not say another word or I swear your arm can drop off for all that I care."

"You do not want to hear how much I desire you."

"Not at all." She finished tying up the bandage and tucked the loose end firmly under the layers. "I should not desire you back. I should not. I cannot help myself, but it shames me to lust after a man I barely know. I do not like being ashamed of myself, but that is what you have done to me."

Captain Carterton strode moodily away from the ward. For every step forward he took, he slid another step back. Yes, he had got Beatrice panting with desire in his arms last night, but she was no closer to agreeing to marry him than before. It was enough to drive a man to drink.

What did he have to do to make her see that he was the man for her, that no other man would do?

He had told her he loved her, and she had thumbed her nose at his declaration of passion. He had shown her desire, and she had acted as if it were of no account. Worse than that, she felt that her passion was somehow shameful, when in reality it was a precious gift, a joy to share with the man who cared so deeply for her.

He would go and see the sergeant-major and pour out his troubles in the ear of his friend. Sergeant-Major Tofts had been around for a long time. Maybe he would be able to give him some good advice on how to win a woman's heart.

He paused midstep as a thought struck him. Sergeant-Major Tofts was not married, and so unlikely to be full of useful advice on how to woo a wife.

No matter. He would go see his friend anyway. Even if his friend couldn't give him any helpful tips, he would be no worse off than he was at the moment.

★ ★ ★

Mrs. Bettina paused for a moment in the door of the private room, looking at the man lying in the bed. So, this was the wounded soldier she was being paid to take care of. His spirits, as much as his body, were in need of nursing, she had been told.

One of his legs was propped up on a pillow. His eyes were shut, but she did not think he was sleeping.

He was just the sort of man her husband would have been, if her husband had lived. Not tall but sturdy and well built, with a craggily handsome face despite his graying hair. A fine figure of a man whatever his age.

Giving herself a little mental shake, she bustled in with the tray of supper she was carrying for him. Her husband, God bless his soul, was long dead and gone. There was no sense in seeing his face in every stray patient who passed through the hospital.

She placed the tray on the bedside table. "I've brought your supper, sir."

He opened his eyes without surprise. She'd known he was just shamming sleep. "Thank you." His tone of voice was bored, listless, as if he had lost the will to live. A dangerous tone of voice for a man lying in a hospital bed to adopt. It meant he was too close to giving up on fighting. And once a patient had given up trying to fight for his life, the doctors might as well sign his death certificate then and there, for he'd be needing it soon enough.

"I'm the private nurse hired to look after you," she explained brightly, as she fluffed up his pillows and helped him to sit up. He looked far too nice a man to be allowed simply to give up on life. "Seems some of your army friends weren't happy with you being in the wards with all the others, and have paid for every-thing nice for you. Anything you need, you just have to ask."

"They're good friends," he said, in the same I-don't-care-about-anything-anymore tone.

Now that he was sitting up, she placed the tray on his lap and shook a linen napkin over him. He made no move to pick up his knife and fork.

She waggled her finger at him. "Now then. You've got to eat to keep up your strength."

With a sigh of defeat, he took a mouthful of stew, chewed and swallowed. "It's good," he said, the first real emotion she had heard from him.

"Of course it is. I made it myself, so I expect you to eat every bite."

Under her watchful gaze, he finished his meal and wiped his mouth in the napkin. "I'll be away now," she said, as she collected his empty tray. "But I'll be back in the morning. If you need anything in the night, you can call one of the night nurses."

"Thank you." Was it her imagination, or was his voice just a little less defeated? Just a little more full of life and vigor?

Bending over, she dropped a light kiss on his forehead, the sort of kiss a mother might give to a sick child. She could not help herself. There was nothing motherly about the feelings she could have for such a patient if she let herself. "Get better," she instructed him. "You have too much to live for to give up on life."

She could feel his eyes boring into her as she walked out of the door.

The sergeant-major was already sitting up in bed when she arrived the next morning—a tray of fresh-baked bread and newly churned butter to brighten up his breakfast. He ate it with relish, his eyes not leaving her the entire time.

On her way in, she had asked a junior nurse to bring her a jug of hot water, a bowl, and some clean towels. The girl brought them in just as he finished eating.

Mrs. Bettina shut the door behind her to give her patient some privacy, then poured some hot water into the bowl and lathered up a washcloth. "How is your leg this morning?"

"Fine," he said brusquely.

So, he didn't want to talk about his wound. Fair enough. It would do him no good to dwell on it anyway. "I am going to give you a bath this morning to freshen you up."

A look of alarm crossed his face. "I don't want a bath," he muttered. "I'm perfectly fine without one."

"Glowering at me won't get you out of it," she said, as she removed the breakfast tray and pulled away the bedclothes.

He was wearing a blue-striped cotton nightshirt that came down past his knees, just showing a pair of fine calves.

She swallowed uncomfortably. He was a finer man than her usual run of patients. It was hardly professional of her to be quite so eager to give him a bath.

"Leave the water here and I will wash myself," he barked at her.

"I am not one of your soldiers," she replied tartly. "You cannot order me around. You are in my domain here, and you have to follow my orders."

"Then get one of the other nurses to give me a bath," he grumbled.

She paused just before beginning to wash the foot of his good leg. "Is there something wrong with me?" She felt unaccountably disappointed that he would prefer someone else to attend to him. Did he not like her around him?

"You are far too . . . too fine a woman to be bathing an old soldier." His ears were a fiery red, and the color crept over his entire face. "It is too personal a task for you to do for me."

His embarrassment made her feel oddly ill at ease, too. "I am your nurse," she replied stoutly, squelching her unease under a veneer of professionalism. "Keeping you clean is one of my duties."

Inside, though, her heart could not refrain from giving a happy warble. He thought she was a fine woman? Even though she was nearly as old as he was? Most men his age would take themselves a twenty-year-old woman as their wife if they could find one and not look twice at someone so near their own age as she was.

He let her wash his good leg, and then change the dressings on his wound without another comment. Only when she lifted his nightshirt to wash his privates did he speak again. "You have never told me your name."

"Mrs. Bettina," she replied, trying to keep her mind on the task at hand. Her patient didn't remind her of her late husband in every area. Even at his best, her husband had never sported such a magnificent appendage at that, which lay quiescent under her hand.

He made a choking noise, and she looked up sharply to check that he was not having a fit.

"Nancy?" he said, as if he couldn't quite believe her. "Nancy Bettina?"

"Who are you?" she asked suspiciously. Few enough people even knew what her Christian name was, let alone dared to address her by it.

"Bartholomew Tofts. Sergeant-Major Bartholomew Tofts."

Mrs. Bettina stopped dead still, holding the washcloth in midair. "You cannot be." She could feel the blood drain from her head and wondered if she was going to faint.

They stared at each other in silence for a few moments. The sergeant-major was the first to break it. "You do not look anything like your photograph." He sounded confused, as if he could not quite work out what was real and what was fantasy.

All the blood came rushing back to her head now and she felt her face start to burn as hot as the inside of her oven. Ever since she had sent him the saucy photograph of Myrtle and pretended it was of her, she had regretted her choice. It had not been fair to the sergeant-major, and she was sure her trick would do her no good in the end.

"I liked writing to you and receiving your letters back again," she mumbled, looking at the washcloth rather than at his face. "I thought you would not be interested in me anymore if you found out how old I was. So I sent you the photograph of a pretty young friend of mine."

"Not interested in you?" He made another choking noise. "I had tried to put you out of my mind, thinking that despite your kind words, you were far too young for a grizzled old soldier like I am. Instead I find that you are a thousand times more beautiful than your photograph. A thousand times more suitable in every way."

She would have suspected his words were flattery, but his body told her he spoke the truth. His member was stirring on its nest of curls, twitching as it grew to an even more prodigious size. She watched it out of the corner of her eye, fascinated. If only she were brave enough to reach out and take him in her hands, to feel the strength of him. It had been so long since she had touched a man that way.

He seemed quite unaware that his nightgown was bunched up around his stomach and openly displaying everything he had to offer a woman. "Did you mean what you wrote in your letters? Or were they just fun to you?" His voice was diffident, almost apologetic.

"I have been widowed a long time," she admitted. "Your letters brought me to life again."

"I thought about you all the time when I was out on patrol, you know. I dreamed of coming back to England to meet you. It was thoughts of you, of your warmth and kindness, that kept me alive when I was lying on the bare veld with my leg shot out from beneath me. Without the dream of meeting you to keep me going, I would have given up."

He had been thinking of her kindly, then? She summoned up all her courage to look him in the eyes again. "You have too many good years left on you to give up."

"Years of loneliness are not worth having." Any trace of animation in his voice had faded. "I've spent my life in the army, ever since I was fourteen years old. I have no wife, no family, no one to care about me—I gave it all up for Queen and Country. And what has the army given back to me?" He gestured pointedly at his wounded leg. "A useless leg and a miserly pension barely enough to keep me from starvation. I may as well just die in hospital and be done with it. I am no use to anyone."

He sounded so hopeless, so full of despair that she just had to give him a reason to keep fighting for his life. Putting down the washcloth, she reached deliberately for his cock. "Some parts of you still work just fine," she said, as she took it in one hand and stroked it gently. Under her gentle touch, its length quickly grew hard. "Some things are still worth living for."

He made a sort of a splutter in the back of his throat at her touch, but he did not voice any complaint or try to move away.

Emboldened, she moved her other hand to cup his balls, to stroke their silky softness.

It was so long since she had felt a man in her hands. Far too long. A woman of her age ought to be beyond such passions, but she was not. She had missed having her husband in her bed. She had missed the touch of him lying next to her all night long, and the sound of his breathing as he slept. She had missed the bulk of him as he moved over her, into her, claiming her as his wife. She had missed the feel of his thick member filling the empty space inside her.

Now, with the sergeant-major's cock in her hand, all her desires came rushing back into her body with the force of a passion long denied. Her breath came short, and she could feel her chest grow hot. Between her legs, an insistent ache started—an ache that longed to take the member in her hands inside her.

The sergeant-major's face was purple and he was breathing in long, shuddery breaths. Another few strokes and he gave a cry as his sperm erupted, shooting up into the air with such force that it sprayed the bed linen. His face was strained with the force of his orgasm and his fingers clutched at the sheets as if he were holding his soul to his body.

Over and over she stroked him until he had no more left to give. Even then, she could not let him go. She still stroked him as his cock slowly deflated once more.

"I must apologize," he said, as soon as he was recovered enough to speak. "It has been a long time since I have been near a woman. I did not mean to lose control like that."

"I meant for you to find some pleasure in my hands," she replied. Her own body was still humming with desire, and she could feel the dampness between her legs. "I am glad you did not mind my forwardness." Reluctantly, she took her hand away from him, giving him one last lingering pat. "The water in the jug will still be warm. I will have to bathe you all over again."

The water *was* still warm. He offered up no protest when she stripped him of his soiled nightshirt and ran the washcloth over his naked body, washing off all evidence of his pleasure.

Even when she was done, he did not ask for a clean nightshirt, and made no move to cover up with the sheets again. Instead, he pulled her to his side. "Come sit with me."

She ought to get on with her work, but it was not every day that she got to spend in the company of such a man. Gladly she took a seat next to him, and made no resistance when he pulled her close to his side.

"I knew from your letters what a treasure you were. I have waited all my life for a woman like you."

His embrace was warm and comforting. It made her feel cherished, looked after. She had spent her life looking after others—not being looked after herself. The feeling made her warm inside. "There is nothing terribly special about me."

"I am a simple man, with plain wants and desires. In my eyes, you are everything a man could ever want."

She allowed her head to sink down onto his shoulder. "You are too kind."

He laid his free hand on her arm. She could read the hesitation in his face. He wanted to touch her, but wasn't sure, even now, how she would take it.

Her breasts were aching for the feel of his hands, his mouth. She reached up and slowly unbuttoned her bodice, allowing her shirt to fall open.

His hand hovered over her, close but not touching. "You do not mind?" His face was lit up like a boy's at Christmastime.

"I want you to."

He laid his hand on her breasts then, and even though she was still wearing a corset and a shift to mute the sensation, she almost died of pleasure. After her husband's death, she had given up hope that any man would touch her in passion again.

Her fingers shaking, she pulled open the ribbons of her corset and tugged down her chemise to free her breasts. She did not care that he was virtually a stranger to her—she wanted to feel his touch on her bare skin.

"You have such full breasts," he breathed.

She arched her back and moaned with pleasure as his fingers found her nipples, teasing them until they had contracted into hard buds of pure desire. He, too, was affected by the heat between them. His cock was stirring again, lifting its proud head off his stomach and growing thick and hard.

The touch of her breasts and the reawakening of his own desire had made him bolder. "Come and straddle me," he begged. "So I can see your beautiful breasts. So I can take them into my hands and bring them to my mouth. I want to lick you all over, starting there."

"But your leg."

"You will not hurt me. You could not hurt me. And even if you could, the plain would be worth the pleasure a thousand times over."

With such an invitation, she clambered on to the bed and

knelt over him, her petticoats bunched around her knees and her thighs cradling his stomach. In this position, her legs were forced open, and the whisper of air that reached her overheated pussy made her gasp. She was open to him. Open and wet and wanting.

She reached behind her and stroked his cock, with long, slow strokes. Hard enough to tantalize him and make him want more, but not enough to make him come. Not yet. She wanted him helpless with desire and desperate for release before she made him come again. She wanted his second orgasm to be even bigger and better than his first one had been.

When he leaned forward and licked first one breast and then the other with deliberate movements, she was undone. This wasn't about him anymore—it was about her and what she needed from him. She was going to make love to the sergeant-major right here in his hospital bed. If she didn't, she would explode.

She tugged her petticoats above her knees, took hold of his hand and guided it between her thighs to where she burned for his touch. She didn't care if he thought she was a wanton—she needed him too badly for thoughts to get in the way.

"You are so wet," he said reverently, as he stroked her gently. "So warm and welcoming. Too good for an old soldier like I am."

She didn't want his gentleness or his reverence, she wanted his passion. She guided his fingers to the entrance of her cunt, and pushed his forefinger inside her. Her muscles fought against the invasion, contracting around his finger, squeezing it.

"You're going to kill me, woman," he said, taking the rhythm from her and pumping his finger in and out of her with increasing enthusiasm.

She rose on to her knees and taking his erect cock in her hand, she gradually lowered herself onto him, until his head was pushing against the entrance to her pussy, demanding admittance.

He thrust his hands under her skirts and told hold of her hips. "Sit on me. Sit on my cock," he begged her, pulling her down on to him.

Slowly she sank down onto him, not stopping until he was embedded fully into her, stretching her as she had never been stretched before.

"God, you're so tight," he grunted, bucking his hips under her. "You almost made me come just from pushing into you. Now ride me as if I were your horse. Ride me, and make me come all over again. Only this time I'm going to come deep inside you."

Though they were both out of practice, they soon found their rhythm. He let her set the pace. Slowly at first she rose and fell on him, withdrawing almost until he slipped right out of her, and then sinking down onto him, forcing his cock so deep into her that it felt as if he would split her down the middle.

She couldn't get enough of him. This was what she had missed for nigh on a decade, the feeling of a man making love to her. She quickened the pace a little. Now that she had rediscovered the passion that had lain dormant inside her, she had to let it go free. If she were to die in this moment, she would die happy, knowing that she had so much still to live for.

On and on she rode him, allowing him no mercy, no let up in the rhythm. She was reaching that elusive peak, she could feel it—the place where her late husband, despite his best efforts, had only ever managed to take her a few times. The sergeant-major was taking here there without even trying.

She was fighting now to hold off her pleasure, not to reach for it. The more she tried to hold it off, the higher the pressure rose, until with a little scream, she felt her muscles convulse into a pleasure she had thought was forever lost to her, the pleasure of coming to orgasm with a man's cock buried deep inside her. Fiercely she rode him then, plunging him into her, milking every last drop of pleasure from his body.

He could not resist her last wild ride. As her pussy clenched him tight, throbbing with satisfaction, he exploded in his turn. His hot semen spurted into her, filling her with the very essence of him.

Suddenly embarrassed now that her desperate need was slaked, she tried to clamber off him again. She could not believe that she had practically ravished one of her patients. She had climbed on top of him and ridden him hard, forced him to fuck her until she came. If anyone in the hospital were to hear of this, she would be dismissed instantly without a reference. She would be lucky if they did not lock her up for corrupting her patient.

He held tight to her under her skirts. "Don't leave me yet," he begged. "I have only just found you."

She relaxed into the comfort of his arms for just a moment. Truly, she did not want to leave just yet. "I cannot stay. I did not bar the door."

Reluctantly he let his grip on her slacken. "I will let you get up just for long enough to straighten your skirts," he reluctantly conceded. "Then you must come back and lie next to me."

She stood back up and surveyed the mess they had made. The bedclothes were lying in a heap on the floor, the pillows had slipped off the end of the bed, and the sheets were wrinkled and hanging half off the bed. If someone were to come in now, they would see at a glance exactly what had been going on. "I cannot loll around next to you all day. I must change your linen, dress you in a clean nightshirt, make you presentable for your visitors."

He caught hold of her hand and brought it to his lips. "Hang the visitors. I don't want anyone but you."

She smiled at the sincerity in his voice. His words warmed her from the inside out. She trailed a finger across his stomach, slick with sweat and semen, then brought it to her lips to taste him. "But first of all I had better give you yet another bath."

Captain Carterton's eyes widened in surprise. Then he pulled the door shut as quietly as he could and tiptoed away down the hospital corridor. The sergeant-major was far too pleasurably occupied to want visitors right now. Despite his bad leg, he had wasted no time in getting into the good graces—and under the skirts—of his buxom new nurse. Judging by appearances, the sly old dog would be occupied for some time yet.

He gave a sigh of frustration and ran his hands through his hair. Even the sergeant-major's love life was more successful than his own. His week of grace was nearly over, and Beatrice was so far proving stubbornly resistant to his every overture. Every single kiss and caress he'd stolen had been bitterly fought for and hard won. And none of them had gotten him measurably closer to the main prize—Beatrice's capitulation.

He was a soldier. A man of action. When he wanted something, he took it. It galled him to be made to cool his heels waiting on her pleasure.

He'd had enough of waiting. He clapped his hat on to his head and stepped out onto the street. It was time to force the issue. The sergeant-major's shenanigans with his private nurse had given him an idea. He knew just what he needed to do.

Ten

That Friday evening Captain Carterton was once again waiting at the gates of the hospital when Beatrice finished her shift. He doffed his hat and then held out his good arm to her. "Let me walk you home."

She hesitated a moment before taking it. He was more of a danger to her than any ruffian lurking on the streets of London.

The effect that he had on her was not diminishing with time, but growing stronger. Each time she saw him, her heart beat faster in her chest, and she could feel her whole body slowly melt under the heat of his gaze. She no longer felt like a woman of flesh and blood, but a pliable creature of potter's clay, with no will of her own but what he allowed her to have.

Ever since he had given her such shameful pleasure in the park, her body had been craving more. Now she knew how the pitiful opium addicts on the streets felt—they would give up anything and everything just for another pipe, another high, another temporary retreat from the reality that only got more grim with every attempt to escape it.

She was a nurse, a professional woman, with a life of her own, her own friends, and a plan for the future that most emphatically didn't include taking a man like Captain Carterton as her lover. She didn't like feeling so caught, so helpless, as if he could mold her into whatever shape he wanted her to be, and she would have no choice but to remain that way.

But when she put her arm into his and he fell into step with her as they walked along the street toward her lodgings, the heat from his body was a powerful persuader. Whenever she was near him, she did not care that she had no resistance to him. That was what scared her most of all.

They had just turned a corner when, to her surprise, he caught her up in his good arm. A couple of passersby looked at them curiously, but made no move to help her.

Initially too surprised to struggle, she clung onto him as he strode over to a hackney cab, pulled up in the street. Only when he wrenched open the door of the hackney, did she collect her wits enough to struggle.

"What are you doing?" she screeched, as he deposited her inside the carriage and clambered in beside her, rapping on the front panel to indicate to the driver to drive on.

"Abducting you," was his not-at-all reassuring answer.

The horses were moving at a sedate walking speed. She launched herself at the door on the opposite side, only to find it locked.

Captain Carterton was lounging back in the seat beside her, his arms folded over his chest, watching her with an amused expression on his face. "I'm a soldier. If I had gone to the bother of capturing you, I was hardly going to make such an elementary mistake as to give you an easy escape route."

She flew at him next, pummeling him with her fists. Why did men always think they had a right to decide what was best for women? If he had asked her to come away with him, she may have been tempted, even against her better judgment, to agree. But to be given no other option but to go along with his daft plans made her furious. "Let me out. I will not be kidnapped. I will not be."

"I don't recall giving you a choice in the matter," he replied calmly, taking a length of silk from his pocket and holding it up threateningly in front of her. "Now, will you stop attacking me, or will I have to tie you up?"

"You would not dare," she hissed at him.

"I kidnapped you," he reminded her.

"You are nothing but a ramshackle soldier," she spat at him. "A rogue. A rake of the worst kind." If he were to tie her up now, she would lose any chance she had of catching him by surprise and getting away. She sank down into the far corner of the carriage and pulled up the blind to see out of the window.

London passed by her eyes, so near and yet so out of reach. "I will lose my respectability," she said, a little more calmly. "I will never be able to hold up my head in society again. And it will all be your fault. Would you have that on your conscience?" Even as she spoke, the thought of what might happen to make her lose her respectability made a blush rush to her cheek and gave her a tingle of anticipation in the pit of her stomach.

"I will not tell tales to the discredit of the woman I intend to marry," he said stoutly. "Your reputation is safe in my hands."

"On your honor as a soldier?" No decent soldier would break such a solemn promise.

"On my honor as a ramshackle soldier, a rogue, and a rake."

She glared at him. He was not taking her or her concerns seriously. Did he not care that if word of this escapade were ever to get out, her life would be in ruins?

If she truly thought she was in physical danger from him, she would fight until her breath left her body, but she knew he would not hurt her. He was no monster to find pleasure in torturing women.

And he *had* sworn to keep her reputation safe. Having her good name sullied was her greatest concern. She would not be forced into a marriage she wasn't sure she wanted. The worst of her fury began to subside. "Where are you taking me?"

"My brother has a cottage by the sea. Nor far from Brighton, actually. We used to take the train down there from London occasionally when we were children. Of course, I couldn't abduct you and put you on the train, so I hired a hackney to take us all the way there instead."

"Your brother will not care that you have kidnapped me?"

He gave an easy laugh. "My brother will never know. He hates the place. The cottage is left empty year round."

The horses were still clip-clopping through the city streets, but they had entered a part of town she did not recognize. Throngs of laboring men in workers' smocks crowded the roadway, fighting for space with men pushing handbarrows or the odd donkey cart. The women among the crowd looked desperately bright and brassy, as if they were hell-bent on making the most of their short time on earth. "How long until we get there?"

He caught her anxious glance out the window. "I wouldn't try to get out of the carriage here. It's a bit of a rough neighborhood. You're safer inside the coach with me."

"What are you going to do with me when we get there?"

"Nothing you will not enjoy."

Even if she could get past him, which she doubted she could, she would not like to be wandering alone in this part of town. "I would like for you to take me home." She made her voice sound as calm and rational as she could. "Unlike you, I am not on leave. I have a job to do. I have no time to play silly games with you. I have to be at the hospital at seven in the morning. If I simply do not turn up, giving them neither notice nor excuse, I will be dismissed."

"This is not a game, Beatrice." He crossed his arms over his chest and looked her squarely in the eyes. "I have been in love with you for months, and yet you refuse to listen to me. You are on the verge of promising yourself to another man even though you do not love him. He is not the man for you and you know it. What else can I do to make you see reason?"

She was uncomfortably aware that it was her fault he was in love with her. If she had not led him on through her letters, she would be sitting down with Mrs. Bettina and the other girls to a hot supper right now, instead of trundling through the streets in a hired carriage on her way to goodness-knows-where. "I am not promised to anyone. I gave you a week to court me, to see if you could change my mind about you." Even to her own ears, it was a feeble excuse.

She did not dare confess to him she had already decided she could not marry Dr. Hyde. At least not while she felt so strongly for the captain. He would take it as a sign that he had won, and she was not ready to promise herself to him, either. She might never be ready.

"I still have a day or two left. And I will command your undivided attention for the whole of that time. When we return to London, I have every confidence that you will agree you belong with me."

"And my position at St. Thomas's? How will you salvage that?"

"As my wife, you will have no need to work. In addition to my captain's pay, I own a small estate in Surrey that I inherited from my grandmother. My brother's steward looks after it. You will not want for anything."

"I *like* my job. I *like* being a nurse."

"You would have to give it up if you were to marry Dr. Hyde, as you seem so set on doing. Why would you not give it up to marry me, when I love you infinitely better than he ever could?"

He did not understand. Part of Dr. Hyde's attraction had been that he understood that medicine was not an occupation, it was a calling. She could just as soon give up breathing or eating. "I would not give up my position to be married to any man." Healing others is what gave her life purpose and meaning.

He looked at her blankly for a moment, then gave his head a bemused shake.

Just then, her stomach gave a loud gurgle. It was past suppertime and she was hungry. Keeping her from her dinner was yet one more sin she could chalk up to his account. At the rate he was clocking up sins, his soul would belong to the devil before tomorrow morning.

He grinned at the noise and pulled a basket out from under their seat. "I'm an old campaigner and I know that an army marches on its stomach. I have come prepared."

Despite her anger with the way he had cornered her, she was grateful to see the food he pulled out. A French tart, fresh crusty bread with a wheel of soft cheese to accompany it, and a couple of pears. There was even a bottle of white wine that was still cold.

He handed her a portion of tart on a napkin. "I'm afraid we have no time to picnic by the roadside. I want to get to the cottage before the light goes."

The tart was so freshly baked it was still warm, and the pastry flaked and melted in her mouth. She washed it down with a glass of the wine. It was stronger than the weak ale she was used to drinking, and combined with the motion of the carriage, it made her head swim.

When she was done, she leaned back into the cushions. For now, she was safer inside the carriage than outside it. Even once they reached the cottage in Brighton, she would hesitate about asking for help and having to deal with the scandal that would ensue. Maybe it would be best to let the situation ride until the captain returned her to London, and count on his conscience to help her deal with the consequences.

For consequences there certainly would be. The matron ran a tight ship. Nurses had been dismissed from St. Thomas's Hospital on far flimsier grounds than unexpectedly not turning up for work for several days. She would have to concoct a believable lie and hope it would be enough to save her position.

He patted his shoulder. "You'll be more comfortable if you lean against me."

Her neck was already getting a crick in it. She shuffled over until she could rest her head on his shoulder. Her eyes started to drift shut. "Wake me when we get there." It had been a long day on her feet, and she had not been sleeping well lately. Thinking about it, she hadn't gotten a decent night's rest ever since Captain Carterton had returned to England. Another sin to add to his tally.

She'd meant her words as a joke, but when she opened her eyes again the carriage had stopped moving and Captain Carterton was gathering her in his arms. Either the cottage was much closer to London than he had admitted to, or she had slept for several hours.

"I'm awake," she murmured sleepily, but he did not put her down.

He carried her through the dark night and into the cottage. She saw no reason to protest. If he was strong enough to abduct her despite his wounded arm, he was strong enough to carry her.

A fire had been lit in the bedroom where he carried her and laid her down on the counterpane. Its cheery crackle lit the room with a dim light. Captain Carterton fetched a taper and lit a gas lamp. "You can sleep here tonight."

She pulled a face. "In my uniform?"

"If you want to. But there will be a clean nightgown and some fresh clothes for the morning in the closet if you would prefer."

A wardrobe of clothes to choose from? The thought disturbed her. "Do you bring many women here?"

His sigh spoke of irritation. "Do you trust me as little as that?"

"You have given me precious little reason to trust you."

"The clothes here belonged to my sister-in-law. They are all clean and of good quality, even if they are no longer in the height of fashion."

"Belonged?" She would not wear the clothes of a person who had died from a sickness. Staying in her uniform was preferable to running the risk of catching tuberculosis or pneumonia.

"She died here. A fall from her horse. That is why my brother never uses the place. He has avoided it ever since her death."

Such stories always made her melancholy. "He must have loved her very much."

"He loved her rather less when he realized she had not been alone in the cottage."

Beatrice gulped. "Oh, I see."

"It's an old story." He shrugged. "I visit the cottage when-

193

ever I am back in England. I was always fond of her. But enough ancient history. Can I heat you some washing water before you retire? Or boil the kettle for a cup of tea?"

He laughed out loud at her look of surprise. "Of course I can make a pot of tea. I am a soldier, not some ninny of a bank clerk who has no notion of life outside his stool in the office. Many's the time in the field I have had to boil my own water and make my own tea or go without."

"Then thank you, yes, I would like a cup of tea."

As soon as he was gone, she rose from the bed and prowled around the room, all trace of sleepiness gone.

The bedroom was plain and sparsely furnished, but clean and comfortable. She drew back the curtain and looked out of the window, but the dark night hid the surroundings from view. She was certainly not in London. There were no street lamps—no lights anywhere in the distance.

It was quiet, too. Quieter than it ever was in London. No carts rumbling noisily across the cobblestones. No night soil men clattering and clanking through the streets. No cries of street vendors or whinnies of horses pulling a too-heavy load. And if she listened closely, she could hear the faraway whoosh and roar of the sea.

She would have to sleep here tonight and see what the morning brought.

She inspected the closet. As Captain Carterton had promised, it was full of clothes. Beautiful clothes, too. Gowns of expensive silk, striped bodices, even a luxurious coat of heavy velvet. She ran her hand over the soft fabric. She'd drooled over a coat like this in a shop window last winter but had been horrified at the cost. Captain Carterton's brother must be wealthy to afford to buy his wife such luxuries.

At one end of the closet hung a few nightgowns. Seeing them, she could well believe that whomever they had belonged to had used the cottage as a place for secret assignations. No sturdy flannels or even plain cotton among them. Just frothy confections of silk and lace that displayed more than they concealed.

She picked the most modest one and laid it out on the bed. Then, opening the door and checking that Captain Carterton was not lurking outside in the hallway, she quickly stripped off her uniform.

The silk went on smoothly over her naked body and floated around her calves. She had never owned anything so decadent as this one nightgown.

She caught a glimpse of herself in the mirror inside the closet. The fabric clung to all her curves, and the thin fabric was so transparent as to be almost sheer. Through it she could see the dusky pink of her nipples and a dark triangle at the apex of her thighs.

Hurriedly she got into the bed and pulled the covers over her. The mattress was filled with soft feathers, and a goose-down comforter was spread over it.

Only just in time. Captain Carterton walked in to the room with a cup of tea on a tray.

He placed it on the bed for her, and then shrugged off his jacket and started to unbutton his shirt.

Wide-eyed, she watched him as she sipped her tea. "This is my room. Go away. Or if you will not go away, then keep your clothes on."

His shirt now unbuttoned, he kicked off his shoes. "I cannot sleep in my clothes."

"I did not ask you to."

He took off his shirt and pulled off his linen undershirt. "This cottage was designed as a love nest. There is only one bedroom. Only one bed."

His chest was broad and smooth. She swallowed uncomfortably as she looked at him, not daring to look away for fear of what he would do next. In her heart she had known it would come to this as soon as he had climbed into the carriage beside her. "You cannot mean to share it with me."

With his shirt now off, he was unbuttoning his trousers. "That is exactly what I mean to do."

She tucked the bedclothes tightly around her body. "I cannot sleep in the same bed as a strange man. You will have to take the floor."

"The floor? When there is a perfectly good feather bed with room in it for me? I do not think so."

He was wearing nothing but his linen smalls now. "You are a soldier, as you keep on reminding me. Surely you have slept in worse places."

"Not when there was something better on offer."

He had better keep his word not to tell tales on her, or her reputation would be utterly ruined. No one would believe that

she had innocently shared a bed with him. She wasn't sure herself that it was possible, but it seemed once again that she had little choice in the matter. "Then, at least, put some clothes on. You are indecent."

"Unlike you," he gave her a huge smile as he pushed his smalls over his hips and let them fall to the floor. "I always sleep in the nude."

When Beatrice still had not arrived home by ten that evening, Lenora went in search of Mrs. Bettina. It was very unusual for her roommate not to be at home so late in the evening. Quite unheard of.

Mrs. Bettina was sitting by the parlor knitting socks and humming to herself. Actually humming. Lenora had seldom seen her look so cheerful. She hated to break into her landlady's mood. "Beatrice is not here," she said baldly, not knowing how to break it to the matron any more gently. "She finished her shift the same hour as I did. She should have been home long before now."

She tried not to show it, but she was worried sick about her friend. Beatrice would surely have told her if she was planning to go out in the evening. Being roommates they always shared such information as a courtesy, so each would know when to expect the other home.

If Beatrice was planning an evening meeting with Dr. Hyde, he might have mentioned something in passing, too. She had been working with him on an operation all the afternoon, and he had had plenty of opportunities to casually allude to his

plans. He knew she and Beatrice were best friends as well as roommates. But he had said nothing.

Lenora had been battling panic all evening. The streets of London were not always safe. Anything could have happened to an unescorted young woman on her way home.

Mrs. Bettina gave her a measured glance. "I would not worry about Beatrice. I saw her leaving the hospital in the company of Captain Carterton. And the sergeant-major told me—" She blushed and cleared her throat. "Sergeant-Major Tofts told me that Captain Carterton was planning a surprise for her this weekend. I wouldn't be surprised if we didn't see her until Monday."

Lenora gaped. "But she is planning to marry Dr. Hyde. She told me so herself. And she doesn't even like the captain very much. I heard her grumbling about how annoying he was just this morning."

Mrs. Bettina would not be disturbed from her knitting. "I think the captain is growing on her."

"But the doctor?"

"The doctor takes her for granted. Maybe a little competition in that quarter will open his eyes to what he really wants."

Lenora retreated to the room she shared with Beatrice— alone. However lightly Mrs. Bettina was taking the absence of one of her lodgers, Lenora herself was not so sanguine. She did not trust Captain Carterton as Mrs. Bettina did.

She had heard Beatrice crying in the night on the evening she had gone to the music hall with the captain. He had clearly

not treated her as a gentleman ought to treat a lady, but had managed to upset her badly. Beatrice never cried.

If Captain Carterton had persuaded or somehow tricked Beatrice into going away with him for the weekend, she could be in all kinds of trouble. Lenora would not be a true friend of hers if she did not try to find her.

She climbed back up the stairs and into bed, but sleep eluded her. She would go and see Dr. Hyde in the morning and tell him of Beatrice's absence. He was a clever man. He would know what to do.

"Did you sleep well?"

The low husky voice roused Beatrice from a light doze. Though the captain had kept to his side of the bed during the night, she had been on edge and had slept poorly. She had lain stiff as a board for much of the night, fearful lest she should roll over and bump into him in her sleep.

The first birds were singing with the coming of the dawn before she had drifted off into a deeper sleep, and even then she had been prevented from truly resting by disturbing dreams. Saucy dreams of passion. Erotic dreams of her limbs tangling with the captain's, of his mouth kissing her privates, of his finger inside her teasing her, bringing her to the brink but not quite pushing her over . . .

She had never slept in the same bed with anyone other than one of her sisters before. Let alone with a man who had made no secret of his desire for her. It was no wonder she had been restless.

She looked blearily up from her mound of pillows. "No, I did not." Yet another sin to add to his tally. "Did you expect I would?"

"You need to relax. Stop worrying so much. Me? I slept like a baby."

She shut her eyes again. "I do not want to know. Are we returning to London today?"

He reached out and brushed a tendril of hair away from her cheek. "Do you love me yet?"

"No."

"Will you marry me anyway?"

She twitched away from his hand. She didn't want his tenderness. "Certainly not."

"Then I'm afraid we will have to remain here."

"Do you intend to keep me here until I agree to your demands?"

"Only until my week is out. You are a smart young woman. By then I am confident you will have seen the merits of my proposal."

"You are mad. Utterly mad." A man would have to be mad to run off with her, determined on making her fall in love with him. It was arrant nonsense.

A woman did not fall in love with a man just because he wanted her to. She fell in love with him because she knew he was of good character. That was certainly the first thing she herself looked for in a man. Everything else was negotiable, but a good character was paramount.

She turned her back on him. "You cannot win my heart this way. And you definitely will not win my hand in marriage."

"Do the two of them not go together?"

"I am a practical woman. I do not ask for the moon and the stars as well."

After all, what did she know about the captain? He was handsome, sure, in a well-cut uniform and moustaches kind of way, but that was only his outside. His inside was so much more important. And all she knew of his character was that he was highly impulsive. That was no recommendation for a husband.

Her brother, Teddy, seemed to like him well enough, but men were notoriously poor judges of character. Or maybe it was simply that the qualities that made a man a good companion were exactly the opposite to those that made him a good husband.

As for his quest to make her fall in love with him? She'd known it was impossible from the beginning. Women did not fall in love at the drop of a hat—he should know better than that. A woman gave up so much on entering the married state that she had to exercise the utmost caution in accepting a man's proposal. Her poor sister Emily had married a brute, and had had to run away from him. At least Emily was happy now, though she had burned her bridges with society and would never be respectable.

Beatrice was greedy—she wanted to be happy and respectable. Marriage to a handsome soldier she had only just met, a captain in the army who was duty bound to serve in whatever far-flung corners of the Empire he was sent, was a recipe for disaster.

But although she did not want to marry him, she could not

pretend he left her indifferent. Love was one thing—but lust, she had recently discovered, was quite another.

She had liked Dr. Hyde well enough to marry him, but she did not want to touch him. Not like she wanted to touch the captain. She wanted to take off all the captain's clothes and run her hands down his body, to savor every inch of it. She wanted to run her hands through his hair, and over his chest. She wanted to feel the muscles on his thighs, and stroke his member until it stood up proud and strong for her. She wanted to feel him on top of her, his body matched with hers, skin on skin.

Even now, lying half asleep in the mound of pillow, she could feel her body responding to his nearness, begging her to act on her fantasies. In between her thighs was prickling with heat, and she writhed uncomfortably on the bed to make the itching go away. It didn't. Her movements only intensified the heat, and made it move across her body. Her chest was hot and flushed now, too, and she could feel her face start to burn.

His eyes darkened as he watched her. "You can fight it all you want, but it's not going to go away."

He knew what she was feeling, the desires that were tormenting her. Perversely, it made her all the more determined to resist him. "It may not go away immediately, but I can ignore it. I can refuse to give in to it."

He moved toward her on the bed, the mattress sinking beneath his weight, drawing her closer toward him. "Why refuse yourself something that you want so much?"

She held herself stiff, refusing to relax into his embrace. He did not deserve her. "For the same reason that I do not eat a pound of chocolate at one sitting. Because it is not good for me, and however much I want to give in to the temptation at the time, I know it would make me feel ill straight afterward."

"I taste better than chocolate."

She turned her head away, fighting temptation. "I would not know."

"Don't you want to taste me?"

"Not at all."

"Like I tasted you in the hansom cab?"

She gave an involuntary jump and turned to face him, her eyes wide. How could a woman do that to a man? "You mean . . . ?" She wasn't quite brave enough to put her question into words.

"Yes, a man likes to have a woman's mouth on him, just as a woman likes to be tasted by a man. Are you not curious to try it?"

What would it feel like to have his cock in her mouth? She had held him briefly in her hand the other night, and had felt how strong and smooth he was. But what would he taste like? Would he like to be licked gently, or would he want to put as much of himself as he could in her mouth, and to have her suck on him?

Whatever he tasted like, she would never know. "You would taste like too much chocolate," she said firmly. "And I do not want to have a stomachache."

He sighed then, a sigh dragged out from the bottom of his soul. "I have been patient with you, Beatrice. More than patient. And I am not, by nature, a patient man."

"I'm sure it is good for your soul for your patience to be tried once in a while," she replied flippantly, turning her back to him again and snuggling back down into the bedclothes. He had abducted her against her will—she saw no reason to entertain him. "After all, you have a lot to atone for."

"But I have run out of patience now." With those ominous words, he pulled her over onto her back, looped a length of silk over her wrist and tied it tight.

There was no point in fighting him—he was stronger than her and would have his way in the end. She merely glared at him while he looped the silk over her other wrist and tied the ends to the bedposts.

She had seen such bonds on severely disturbed patients who were so out of their minds they were a danger to themselves or to their caregivers. Never had she imagined that one day she would find herself tied up in such an undignified fashion, totally helpless, unable to move, unable to protect herself, unable to have any will of her own. Trust the captain to seek to impose his will on her in such a manner.

"Tying me up will do you no good," she said calmly, as he pulled back the covers and looped similar lengths of silk around her ankles, spread-eagling her on the bed. "I am not a dog to be chastised."

When he had finished, he stood back and looked at her, his naked body standing proud in the early morning sunshine. "I won't hurt you."

"Let me go." Secretly she did not want him to let her go.

Secretly she wanted to stay tied up like that, powerless to resist him. The thought that he could do whatever he wanted to her and she would not be able to resist him made her prickle with wet between her legs. She wanted him to take her like that, to thrust his cock into her while she lay helpless, unable to prevent him . . .

"I can't do that. Not yet."

"What are you going to do to me?" She didn't need to ask, but she wanted to hear him say it out aloud. She wanted to hear the words on his lips.

"Nothing that you don't want me to do."

"I *want* you to let me go," she lied, as convincingly as she could.

"You will be begging me to make love to you before I am done with you."

She would stay tied up for a week before she humbled herself in front of him. "I will never beg you. Never. I would rather die."

His only answer was a grin, a look of truly devilish delight. "I consider that a challenge. I'm a soldier. I love challenges."

Dr. Hyde was not rostered on duty at the hospital the next morning. The matron on the wards gave Lenora a suspicious glare when told the matter was urgent. "Can't it wait until tomorrow?"

Lenora stood her ground. When matters called for it, she had a backbone of steel and nerves of iron. She could outface even the scariest matron when the safety of her best friend was at stake.

Five minutes later she was back on the street, the direction to Dr. Hyde's lodgings clasped tightly in her hand.

He lived in handsome lodgings close by St. Thomas's. A maid

opened the door and ushered her into a pretty parlor as Lenora explained the urgency of her message. There she sat, twisting her hands together and staring at the flocked wallpaper as she waited for him to make his appearance.

It seemed an age before he strode into the parlor. The room seemed to shrink to half its size when he came in. He was so strong, so male. His hair was so freshly washed and combed it was still wet, and he was still buttoning his shirtsleeves. "What is it, Miss Coppins? Has something happened at the hospital?"

She gulped. Seeing him in his shirtsleeves was so intimate. Almost wifely. She had to look away until he had shrugged on his jacket. "No, everything is fine there. It's Beatrice."

His eyes took on a guarded look. "Well?" he demanded, when she did not immediately start speaking again.

Now that Dr. Hyde was standing in front of her, she did not know quite how to tell him. "I think she is in some kind of trouble."

While she was speaking his face had turned an interesting shade of pale. "Trouble? What sort of trouble do you mean?"

"She did not come home last night. I know something bad must have happened to her because she is always at home by ten o'clock at the latest. She is not the sort of girl . . . not the sort of girl who . . ."

"Did she give you no indication of where she was?"

"I told Mrs. Bettina that Beatrice was missing, but she told me not to worry." Now that she had found her voice she could not stop talking. "She said that the sergeant-major she looks after had said something about Captain Carterton preparing a surprise for Beatrice this weekend, and not to worry if we didn't see her until Monday. But Beatrice mentioned nothing to me about being away, and she was due to start work this morning. It didn't seem right to me. Not when she and you . . ."

Her voice finally trailed off in embarrassment. It was harder than she thought telling Dr. Hyde all she knew. What if he were to blame Beatrice for the situation? But no, he was a fair man. He would not harbor a grudge, or blame Beatrice for something that was not her fault. "I thought I'd better come to you and tell you what had happened. I knew that you'd know what to do."

The longer she spoke, the more agitated he became. "You have done right to fetch me," he said, when she eventually ran out of breath. "You say that one of the patients at the hospital knows what might have happened?"

"I should have stopped by and asked him when I was at the hospital, but I didn't think of it," Lenora confessed. "I only thought of finding you as soon as I could."

"Walk back with me. We shall go and interrogate the sergeant-major together."

Lenora fell into step beside him on the street. With his coat and hat on, and carrying a cane in his free hand, he was every inch the gentleman.

If she had been the woman lucky enough to engage his attention, she would have fought to the death rather than allow herself to be taken away by another man. But Beatrice did not yearn for Dr. Hyde as she did. Nobody could yearn for Dr.

Hyde as earnestly as she did. Beatrice did not burn in the night for the touch of the doctor's hands on her body, or spend her daytime hours dreaming about the feel of his lips on hers.

No, Lenora feared that Beatrice burned for the touch of the captain instead.

Lenora waged a war within herself. Was it disloyal of her to her friend to hint to the doctor that maybe Beatrice did not love him as he deserved to be loved? She cared for Beatrice dearly, but was it quite fair to Dr. Hyde for Beatrice to marry him if she did not love him?

Even if Dr. Hyde adored Beatrice—and she could understand why he would—wouldn't it be better for him to wait until he found a woman who really cared for him in return? Wouldn't it be better for Beatrice, too, to marry a man she truly wanted?

Lenora did not harbor any illusion that the doctor would turn to her for consolation if Beatrice were to leave him. She was plain-featured, not pretty like Beatrice was. Her mouth was too wide, and her hair was far too red. Her hips were too plump and her bosom was ridiculously generous. She was too earthy to be any man's ideal wife.

No, Dr. Hyde would never love her as she loved him. But there were other women in the world who might love him as much as he deserved, even if they couldn't love him quite as much as she did.

In the end, she decided it would be wisest to hold her tongue. If Dr. Hyde had not worked out for himself that Beatrice did not really care for him, she did not want to be the bearer of bad news. Worse still, Dr. Hyde might think she spoke out of jeal-ousy and not out of love for both of them. She could not bear for him to think badly of her.

She would have to stand by watching and waiting, and hope that no lives—not Beatrice's, not Dr. Hyde's, and not her own—were ruined in the muddle.

Eleven

Beatrice lay tied on the bed as the Captain walked around her, just looking at her.

"Your nightgown is bunched up underneath you. You would be more comfortable if I were to take it off."

She stayed silent, trying not to look at him too obviously. She'd not seen him naked before, and he was well worth a second look. His chest was broad and strong, and his arms were tanned a golden brown from the South African sun. His thighs were thick and strong, his buttocks were firm but full, and his member stood up proudly from its nest of curls. If her hands had been free, she would have wanted to touch it.

"I shall take your silence as consent," he said easily. Bending over her, he took the edges of her nightgown in his hands and pulled.

The fabric ripped all the way to her neck with a screech. He pulled the torn pieces from under her and tossed them on to the floor. "I trust that is more comfortable?"

He made her feel as though she was spread out like a meal on a table, waiting to be feasted upon. How could any woman be comfortable tied up to the bedposts with a man staring at her as if he wanted to eat her. She merely looked at him without bothering to answer.

It would be easier to deal with him if only she did not want him so much. If she was indifferent to his touch, she could shut him out of her mind and pretend he did not exist, whatever he did to her. But she was not indifferent. And she could not ignore him.

"I never heated you any water for washing last night," he continued in a conversational tone. "I shall have to remedy that lack right away."

Still stark naked, he strode out of the bedroom. She could hear the sound of a match being struck and water being poured into a kettle.

Before long, he was back in the room with a large basin of steaming water and a washcloth. "I'm afraid I cannot untie you and allow you to wash yourself, but you will find that I make a good body servant."

Setting the basin of water down on the floor, he dipped the washcloth in it and brought it to her body. The water was pleasantly warm against her skin and she gave a little shiver as the drops ran down her body.

"Is it too cold?" he asked solicitously, as he ran the washcloth over her stomach. "Shall I heat the water a little more?"

"You shouldn't be doing this," she muttered, in a desperate

attempt to stave off the temptation of giving in to him, of letting him love her just this once and to hell with any possible consequences.

He gave her a wide-eyed look of mock innocence. "You prefer being dirty?"

"That is not what I meant," she wailed. "You always twist my words around to suit yourself. Of course I do not want to be dirty."

"Then lie still and let me wash you."

"Do I have any other option?"

He stood back and looked at her again. "No, I'm afraid you don't."

It was actually quite pleasant having him attend to her just as she attended to her patients. If she could overlook the fact that her nurse was both naked and obviously male she might even have enjoyed it. But her nerve endings were on edge. Every stroke of the washcloth felt like a caress. He made her feel as though he were not washing her, but loving her.

By the time he put down the washcloth and proclaimed himself satisfied with her state of cleanliness, she was shaking. He had touched her everywhere, everywhere, on the pretext of washing her, and she could not stop him.

She needed him so badly she was almost ready to give in to his demands. If only he would simply take her, and not bother to ask. Then she would not, could not deny him. "Untie me," she begged.

He put the washcloth back in the basin and sat down next to

her on the bed. With his good arm, he reached over and lightly stroked one of her breasts. "Will you marry me?"

"I cannot marry you. Marriage is forever. I do not know you well enough to tie my future to yours."

"By the end of the day you will know me very well indeed, I promise you. Will you agree to marry me then?"

"No." She almost screamed the word in her frustration. "You cannot expect it of me."

"Then I'm afraid I cannot untie you just yet." He moved his hand to stroke between her thighs. "And I'm not sure you really want me to untie you. You like being at my mercy. Feel how wet you are here."

"I am not," she protested. "You are imagining it." But she knew she was wet. She could feel her juices slowly oozing out of her body and onto the sheet underneath her. If she were to move, there would be a damp stain beneath her.

"Not wet?" He swung his legs onto the bed and came to kneel between her legs at the foot of the bed. Then he bent his head until she could feel his breath on her pussy. "You are sopping wet, my love," he informed her. "Positively dripping. Here, shall I show you?" With that, he slid one of his fingers right into her and drew it out again.

She shut her eyes, not wanting to see the evidence of her desire glistening on his fingers.

That did not stop him. He drew his finger across her stomach, leaving a trail as he went. "See?" he whispered, though her eyes were still shut tight.

"I think you want me to taste you again. I think you want me to lick you down there, and make you even wetter. Is that what you want?"

There was nothing left in her to say no, but her mouth refused to frame a yes. All she could do was give the tiniest of nods.

He saw it, as she knew he would. He bent his head again, and blew gently on her pussy. The air was cold where she was wet and she shivered.

He leaned in closer, just touching her with the tip of his tongue.

The sensation was too much for her composure. She arched her back and screamed, not sure if she wanted him to continue or to stop.

"Do you want to taste me, too?" Without even waiting for an answer, he moved his body until they were top and tailing.

She did want to taste him, but his cock bobbed just out of reach of her mouth. "Come closer," she murmured.

"Ah, so the lady has a tongue after all," he teased her. "What did you say? I didn't quite hear you."

"Come closer," she repeated, no louder than before.

Obligingly he moved closer so she could move her head up and take him into her mouth.

She wanted to hold him, to look at him, to examine him, to run her hand up and down him, but having him in her mouth came a pretty close second. She could not see him, but she could examine him with her tongue, feeling each ridge and hollow of his shaft, luxuriating in the smoothness of the engorged head, and tasting the salty drop that leaked out at the very tip.

In return he was exploring her in the same way, until she felt as if she would die of the twin delight of both giving and receiving pleasure.

It was not long before she felt her need start to peak. He was going to give her pleasure, just as he had in the hansom cab. Her breath grew short and her whole body stilled as she felt her orgasm approach.

Right at the critical moment, he drew his head away from her. She made a muffled noise of protest, but she could not stop him.

"I don't think I will let you come just yet," he said, as he moved to straddle her. "Not until you give me what I want in return."

"You can't stop now," she protested. Her whole body felt bereft. Her pleasure was so close, and yet so impossibly far away now.

"*I* am not going to stop. *I* am going to come. And you are going to watch me." With that, he took his cock in his hand and started to stroke it.

She could only watch him helplessly as he pumped himself slowly at first, and then harder and harder.

She could only watch helplessly as he shut his eyes, threw his head back, and took in a deep shuddering breath.

She could only watch as his cock erupted with his seed, spurting it all over her stomach and her breasts.

He milked himself of everything that was in him with a shudder of delight as she watched him, hating him and wanting him in equal measure.

With a groan of utter satisfaction, he lay down next to her, idly rubbing his come over her skin. "What a mess I have made," he murmured softly. "I shall have to give you another bath."

Lenora followed Dr. Hyde as he strode into the sergeant-major's private room. "I believe you might know something of the whereabouts of my fiancée, Miss Clemens," the doctor said without preamble. It was not a question. "She has gone missing."

The sergeant-major shrugged, unperturbed at having his peace disturbed so early in the morning and with such abruptness. "Your fiancée? May I be the first to offer you my congratulations on your engagement."

A hint of red tinged the doctor's cheek. "Miss Clemens has not officially agreed to marry me yet, but I am expecting an answer in the affirmative."

The sergeant-major stroked his moustaches thoughtfully. "I see. And if I do know where she is?"

Dr. Hyde muttered something highly uncomplimentary under his breath about soldiers in general and this soldier in particular. "Then I would be obliged if you would tell me where she is without delay."

"Why?"

Dr. Hyde looked him square in the eye. "So I can go find her and bring her home."

The sergeant-major was silent for a moment. Lenora was just about to add her own pleas to Dr. Hyde's command when he spoke. "I believe she is with Captain Carterton at a cottage in

Brighton. I have the direction if you want it. But I would suggest caution. You might not like what you find there."

Dr. Hyde's lip curled. "Though I am not a soldier," he spoke the word with disdain, "I'm sure I will be able to handle whatever I see. I'm not afraid of any man. The direction, if you please."

With a face that spoke of his deep unease, the sergeant-major rattled off the direction. "Do not underestimate the captain," he added. "Or you may well regret it."

Dr. Hyde gave him a terse nod, turned on his heel, and left without another word.

Lenora stayed just long enough to whisper some thanks to the old soldier in the bed and then she scurried after the doctor.

"I have hired a hackney cab to get us there." Dr. Hyde's voice was terse. "It will take several hours by road."

"Us?" She had done her duty by telling him. What else could he possibly need her for?

"I will need you to come with me. Miss Clemens may need you. You will help to safeguard her reputation on the journey home."

And who would safeguard her reputation on the journey to Brighton? she thought, with a touch of irritation. Dr. Hyde was not usually so blind to the proprieties.

"You will be the perfect chaperone. After all, who could suspect *you* of doing anything that was not perfectly appropriate," he added.

The warmth and approbation in his voice was all it took

for her irritation to melt away like butter under a hot sun. Of course she would go with him to rescue Beatrice. For him, she would do anything.

If Beatrice had thought the first time the captain bathed her was a torment, the second time was a million times worse. He lingered over her body, smoothing the washcloth over her then covering the part he had washed with kisses.

From her toes to her thighs, her fingers to her shoulders, and her neck to her stomach, no part of her escaped his attention. Except the part she wanted him to touch most. He scrupulously avoided touching her there.

It wasn't fair. He had orgasmed all over her, his hot seed covering her body, and she was left on fire, still wanting.

"I must be clean enough to eat dinner off," she grumbled, hiding her arousal behind a show of irritation.

"Now there's an idea. Why didn't I think of that?"

"Don't be silly. And please, take these ties off me. I am getting a cramp."

"Just a little longer. A very little longer." He took up the washcloth for the last time and drew it gently between her legs. The rough fabric clutched at her sensitive skin, and she arched her back with a cry.

"You're almost ready to beg me, aren't you?" he murmured, as he took the washcloth away and replaced it with his mouth, licking her folds lovingly.

She *was* almost ready to beg him. "Undo me. Please," she

said, as he flicked her nub with the tip of his tongue. She could not take much more of his torment.

Then his finger was inside her and she moaned aloud. "Yes, please."

"This isn't the only place a man can take a woman," he said conversationally, as he plunged his finger inside her and drew it our again. He drew it down her privates until it rested against her back passage. "A man can take a woman here, too. Like this." He pushed gently, and the tip of his finger slipped inside her ass. "Would you like me to take you there, Beatrice? Would you like to feel my cock in your ass?"

His finger felt huge inside her. "It would never fit," she panted, feeling her body stretch to accommodate him.

"Oh, I think it would." As he spoke, he pushed his finger inside her further. "I might have to push hard, but you would take all of me eventually. The whole length of my cock. You've made me hard again just thinking about it."

He withdrew his finger and pushed it in again, bringing her to a fever pitch of excitement. "Would you like me to fuck you there? In that forbidden place? I could come in there like I came on your breasts."

She would let him fuck her there, anywhere, so long as he made her come. She could not bear it if he found pleasure in her body and allowed her none in return. "Untie me," she cried, thrusting against his hand. "Please, untie me."

At last he took notice of her pleas. Leaving her panting with need, he reached out and snapped the thin silk of her ties one by one. "Get on your hands and knees, Beatrice."

Her body was free, but her mind was still in thrall to him. Clumsily, she got to her hands and knees as he ordered her to do. Mindless with desire, she had no will of her own left anymore.

He spread her legs apart and bent his head to the cleft between her thighs. He was going to torment her again, and not let her come. "No, please," she sobbed into the pillows. "I cannot take any more."

He took no notice of her protests, instead licking her with a long slow caress of his tongue over her swollen lips. The wetness of him, the softness of his tongue tantalized her beyond bearing. He could have brought her to orgasm a thousand times by now if he had been kind, but he refused to do so. He only wanted to tease her, torment her until she could not breathe.

Though she screamed and bucked to get away from his torture, he held her firm.

"Don't you like being licked?" His voice was low with desire and she could feel his breath tickle the hairs on her mound. "I thought every woman liked the touch of a man's tongue on their pussy."

"No, please," was all she could force past her panting lips.

"No, stop?" He gave her another lick. "Or please continue? You have to be clearer in telling me what you want."

"Please stop."

"Stop licking you? Or stop touching you? Or stop making love to you."

She could not resist him any longer. If he wanted her to beg him, then beg him she would. "Stop licking me and make love to me. Please," she added as an afterthought.

"Make love to you?" He sat back on his heels and held her haunches in his hands. "And how do you propose I make love to you? With my eloquent words? With pretty speeches? With vows of undying love?"

The vows of undying love could come later. "With your body. Make love to me with your body. Fuck me."

"Ah, now we are getting somewhere." His voice was thick was satisfaction at her capitulation. He slid his index finger into her cunt, and then withdrew it slowly. "Is this what you want? Do you want me to fuck you with my finger?"

She was so wet that his finger slid easily into her virgin cunt, stretching it to take his invasion. But although his finger inside her felt divine, it did not fill the emptiness inside her. "No, it is not what I want." She almost screamed at him in frustration. He was not going to leave her with a single shred of pride, but would force her to spell out what she wanted. "I want you to fuck me with your cock, not with your finger. I want you to put your cock inside me. I want you to put your cock inside my pussy and fuck me until I come. Is that clear enough for you?"

"Perfectly clear, thank you. But I think you should ask me nicely, not scream at me like a Covent Garden fishwife."

"Please fuck me," she cried more softly this time, wriggling her rump at him in invitation. "I know your cock is big and hard and stiff and longing for a taste of my pussy. Don't make me wait any longer, I beg you. I want you. You have won—you know you have won. Be generous in your victory and fuck me now."

"I never could refuse a lady when she asked me nicely. I'm going to fuck you now, Beatrice, and make you my woman. You want that, don't you."

"Yes, I want it. You know I do."

Then came the feeling that she had been waiting for all her life. His cock, thick and hard, probed the entrance to her pussy, pushing apart her folds, demanding entrance.

She gasped as he spread her apart with his fingers, readying her for the invasion that was to come. In just a moment she would no longer be a virgin, she would have sacrificed it all for desire.

There were no regrets, not a single one, just a burning need to have him fill her.

Slowly he pushed into her, stretching her with the width of his member. Her muscles contracted, fighting against the alien intruder, but little by little they relaxed as he continued his quest.

He was barely inside her when he stopped. "Your maidenhead," he murmured. "I will dispose of it in the way of a soldier." And with one powerful thrust he broke through and sheathed himself to the hilt inside her.

She felt only a brief pang at the breaching of her maidenhead, and that little bit of discomfort was quickly swallowed by the growing need for fulfillment that was taking over her. If she had thought before that having him thrust his cock inside her would take away the desperate need in her blood, she was wrong. It took her desire to a new level, to a pitch so high she could not bear it.

He withdrew a little way, and she pushed her hips back to urge him back inside her. "Yes, fuck me," she urged him. "I want you back inside me. All the way inside me."

"You like it, don't you?" he said, as he entered her again in a long, slow thrust. "I knew you would like it. Even though you tried to deny it, I knew you were starving for the feel of a man's cock buried deep in your cunt."

"Yes, I like it." She was weeping with need now. "I like your cock inside me, filling me. I will do anything you want as long as you promise you will not stop." He had to let her come. She was so very close. So very, very close . . .

Lenora stood in the doorway of the cottage, not able to believe what she was hearing, what she was seeing. Beatrice, her roommate and best friend, was naked on her hands and knees moaning with pleasure as a man thrust his huge member into her from behind.

It was too much for her. She could not look, but grasped the arm of her companion for support.

He was no help to her. He simply stood stock-still, his eyes wide with shock at the sight of his almost-fiancée being pleasured by a naked stranger. His face had turned an odd shade of gray and his hands were shaking.

She nudged him, afraid that he would have an apoplexy if he stood there any longer. "Dr. Hyde," she whispered. "We should leave." They were intruding on a private moment. Far too private to be shared with others.

He did not move. It was as if he were rooted to the spot with utter horror. "Beatrice?" His voice was a mere croak.

Neither Beatrice nor her paramour heard him, too noisy in their pleasure to take heed of what was going on around them. The captain was pumping into Beatrice, telling her how much she wanted him inside her, how she longed for the feel of his cock, how she needed every inch of him.

Far from disagreeing with him, Beatrice, polite, refined Beatrice, was crying out for him to fuck her, panting how much she loved his cock thrusting into her pussy, and begging him to let her come.

Lenora tugged at his arm a little harder. "We have to leave." She could feel her face starting to blotch with embarrassment, and her armpits were prickling with sweat. How could he stand there watching them when they were so intimately engaged? She wanted to crawl away and hide under a rock before they noticed her.

The couple in front of them were building up into a crescendo of passion. The captain's hips were pumping into Beatrice at a furious rate and she was thrusting back to meet him.

Still Dr. Hyde would not move. Lenora could only watch as the captain plunged into Beatrice one last time with a cry wrung from his soul. He held himself there, his whole body still and contorted, as Beatrice writhed under him, pushing herself against him as if she couldn't get enough.

Then her body, too, went rigid, and she screamed as the force of her orgasm overtook her. Her scream went on and on until Lenora was sure she could not have a breath left in her body. Only then did Beatrice's cry subside into faint defeated sobbing.

The captain withdrew his cock, limp now, but with his semen still dripping from the head. Lenora could not take her eyes off it. Even flaccid, it was an awesome sight. She stole a quick glance at the doctor, wondering if he possessed such a prodigious tool. Unfortunately she did not think she would ever find out.

The captain seemed to sense her scrutiny. At any rate, he turned his head and caught the pair of them standing in the doorway, their mouths gaping open like a fish.

He swore under his breath and swung his legs off the bed. Beatrice looked back over her shoulder to see what the matter was. Her face turned as red as a beet, she made a strangled noise of horror, and sunk to the mattress and buried her face in the pillows.

The movement broke Dr. Hyde out of his seeming trance. He grabbed Lenora by the upper arm and whirled around. "Let's get out of here," he spat, his voice dripping with disgust. "Before your innocence is sullied by the actions of those two . . . those two fornicators."

Lenora allowed herself to be led away. She had no desire to bear witness to her friend's shame. It was bad enough that she had seen Beatrice's nakedness, and the way in which the captain had violated her body.

Temptation

Dr. Hyde strode back to the carriage muttering under his breath the whole way. "I would never have believed it of her. Never. If I had not seen it with my own eyes, I would have thought it was a tall tale, related purely to discombobulate me."

Lenora would have tried to comfort him if he had needed comforting. But to her eyes, he did not seem heartbroken by the incontrovertible evidence of Beatrice's infidelity. Instead, once his initial shock had worn off, he seemed more confused than angry, as if his view of the world had suddenly been proven wrong and he had nothing with which to replace it.

Beatrice huddled on the bed with the bedcovers wrapped around her to hide her nakedness. How could she have gone from the height of ecstasy to the depths of despair in the space of a heartbeat?

It was bad enough that she had given in to Captain Carterton's seduction and had begged him to make love to her. Having an audience for her degradation was a thousand times worse. For that audience to be made up of her best friend, Lenora, and Dr. Hyde, the man she had once planned to marry, was worst of all.

She wanted to hit out at the captain for daring to think of her, for daring to love her. From the moment she had met him, she'd known he would ruin her.

He came and sat beside her on the bed and put his arm around her shoulders in a gesture intended to comfort her. Though his top half was still bare, he had pulled on a pair of trousers to cover his legs. "They have left now."

She shrugged, saying nothing. It didn't matter if they were to stay or to go. They had seen enough to damn her.

"He is not the man for you. If he had truly loved you, he would have stayed and fought for you."

"Even after finding me in another man's arms?" She gave a bitter laugh. There was no joy left in her. It had all been sucked out of her, leaving her dry and withered like an autumn leaf. She didn't care about Dr. Hyde. Truth to tell, she never really had. But she cared deeply about being caught fornicating like a common harlot.

"Especially after finding you in my arms." His arm tightened around her shoulders, constricting her, controlling her.

She pushed it away. "Caught in the very act of fucking another man? No one could overlook that."

"You had promised him nothing. There was no betrayal in our love."

"Love?" She spat the word. "Today has been about many things, but none of them are love. Lust and desire. Control. Possession. But not love." It shamed her that she had not been stronger, that she had let a man who was not her husband take her virginity. She wanted him to feel part of her shame.

Her words found their intended target. He sat up as stiffly as she was. "I cannot speak for you, but there was love on my side. There has always been love on my side for you."

"If you loved me as you profess, you would not have been so sure about what I wanted. You would not have forced a decision on me. You would have given me a choice whether or not to be with you, not taken my choices away."

"But you are not made for Dr. Hyde." The captain ran one hand through his hair with evident frustration. "He would not make you happy. Why is this so clear to everyone but you?"

"This is not about Dr. Hyde. It is about me. Whether or not I am happy is nobody's business but my own. The choice was mine to make and you conspired to take it away from me. You knew I could not resist you.

"Even if he had not come to find me—" Her voice broke, but she cleared her throat and forced herself to continue. "Even if he had not come to find me, I could never have married him after I had been polluted by your touch."

"Is that what you think of me? That my touch has polluted you?" His voice came out sounding as if she had just punched him in the stomach.

She did not care if her words hurt him. He deserved to know what he had done. "I am no longer fit for a respectable man to marry. You have ruined me, as I knew you would."

"I love you, Beatrice. I have loved you since the first letter you sent to me and I saw the goodness in your heart." He sounded helpless now. Hopeless. His cocky smile and his jaunty stride were gone. "But I do not know the Beatrice who is sitting next to me now. She is not the woman I thought I loved."

"You never knew me. You fell in love with a fantasy. I am a woman of flesh and blood, with my own thoughts, my own feelings, my own hopes and dreams."

"I have tried to win your heart in return, but you do not have the generous soul I imagined. You will not let me in."

She was silent. There was nothing more to say.

In the teeth of her silence, he got up and strode around the room. "I am weary of trying to win your affections. Maybe you are right. Maybe I did fall in love with a fantasy."

She should have felt triumphant, vindicated, but all she felt was a hollow ache inside her where her heart ought to have been.

"I will have you taken back to London, back to your boardinghouse, back to your precious Dr. Hyde. He may even take you back again if you play your cards carefully. But I will not be calling on you again. I am out of patience, out of hope, and my soul is weary with being rejected."

"So, this is the end?" She had expected something more dramatic. Tears at least. Arguments, shouting, pleading. Not this dull resignation. "We are through with each other?"

"If you wish to see me again, I would be happy to hear from you, but I will not try to contact you anymore. I am done pursuing you. It is no use. The next move will have to come from you."

She huddled tighter into the bedclothes. Even Captain Carterton was rejecting her. Now that she had succumbed to his seduction and he had taken her virginity, he had no more use for her. He must despise her as a wanton woman, as she despised herself. "That would be for the best," she agreed in a small voice.

This way they would have a clean break. She would not put herself in his power again.

Twelve

"You are no longer required at this hospital."

Beatrice quailed under the matron's steely gaze. "What is the matter? What have I done wrong?" Had Dr. Hyde been so small-minded and petty as to tell the entire hospital what he had witnessed? Even though the story hardly resounded to his credit, either? Few men would willingly confess that their sweethearts found them wanting and had turned to another man to give them satisfaction in bed.

The captain certainly had given her the satisfaction he had promised. Her face burned at the remembrance of how she had been set on fire by his touch. Even now, when she was receiving a dressing-down from the matron, her mind kept wandering back to the cottage by the sea. Captain Carterton had been such a skilled lover in the way he had tormented her until she was almost out of her mind with need, and then fucked her until she had almost passed out with pleasure.

The matron's face had turned slightly pink and her voice grew frostier than ever. "I do not intend to repeat the whole sordid story. Suffice to say that your services are no longer required. St. Thomas's Hospital expects all its nurses to be women of the very highest respectability. Members of our profession already walk a fine line in the eye of society. We cannot afford to let the actions of a few taint the reputations of the rest of us."

It must have been Dr. Hyde who told on her. It had to have been Dr. Hyde. She knew that Lenora would never have betrayed her in that way. "But I have worked here for five years. You cannot just turn me out on my ear like that."

The matron's square face took on a gleam of satisfaction. "I think you will find, Miss Beatrice, that I can do exactly that."

She could not leave her position without putting up a fight for it. "But . . ."

"And do not bother asking for a reference. I would not write anything about your . . . your habits that any prospective employer would want to read. I would make sure that no one else would, either. Now be gone with you." She flapped her apron at Beatrice as if she were a marauding chicken. "We don't want your sort hanging around here and giving the hospital a bad name."

Beatrice turned on her heel and walked away from the woman's gloating smile before she said something that she would regret. The old bat probably hadn't been touched by a man for forty years and was jealous that Beatrice had gotten something she hadn't. The dried-up old prune of a woman. She needed a good hardy man in her bed at night to put her in a better temper with the world.

As soon as she was out of sight, she leaned against the wall and put her head in her hands. So, her career was now in ruins. She would never find another job as a nurse in London now—her reputation would catch up with her wherever she went. That was just what she needed. Her personal life was a disaster, and now her professional life was completely wrecked as well. Could she not do anything right?

The first thing to do, she decided, was to see if she could make amends, professionally at any rate, with Dr. Hyde. He was a reasonable man and had been fond of her once. Before he caught her in a compromising position with another man, true, but maybe he would find some shred of kindness in his heart for her. If he wanted to, he could rescind the matron's dismissal of her. He was a doctor, after all, and she was just the matron.

She strode right into Dr. Hyde's office where she knew she would find him before he started on his ward rounds for the day. "Matron Baddeley just told me I no longer have a job," she announced, with no preamble at all. "I have been dismissed."

He did not look up from his papers. "And you are surprised? After you absconded with your lover instead of coming to work, with no notice to anyone where you were or when you would be returning? She was well within her rights to dismiss you. I saw no reason to interfere with her decision."

The calm in his voice infuriated her. Had he never cared for her at all that he could throw her to the wolves so easily, without batting an eyelid? "You told her I had absconded with my lover? When you knew it wasn't true?" Her voice was rising to a dangerously high pitch and she stopped for a moment and swallowed to regain her self-control. "That was low of you."

"I had to give her some explanation of your absence. Out of kindness to you, I chose an expurgated version of the truth. You should be thankful that I spared her all the gory details."

"I am surprised that you would act in such a petty way and go telling tales on me to the whole hospital. I thought you were my friend."

He put down his pen then, crossed his arms, and fixed her with a glare. "And I am surprised that you dared to show your face here at all. I had thought you were a sensible woman, but no sensible woman would have done what you did." He gave a shudder of distaste. "Or have the gall to turn up to work here as if nothing had happened. And then dare to come and complain to me, the wronged party in all of this, that you no longer have a position to come back to. Truly, your effrontery knows no bounds."

"Captain Carterton abducted me. I did not go with him willingly."

"You forget—I was there. I saw you both. I heard you."

"I did not mean to give in to him."

"Your good intentions did not take you very far."

He had not offered her a seat, but she sat down on the chair opposite his desk anyway. "I always meant to marry you, you know, even though Captain Carterton was so insistent in his attentions to me. You would have made a good husband."

A muscle in his eye twitched, but he gave no other sign of emotion. "Then I am glad you delayed your decision so there is no engagement for us to break. Awkward explanations might have been needed."

"You would not consider marrying me now. Not after . . ." She did not mean it to be a question but a statement of fact. To tell the truth, she could not ever imagine marrying him now—not after the captain had loved her with such passion.

Looking at the doctor in front of her, his mouth pursed in disapproval, she did not know why she had ever considered the possibility so attractive. Yes, he would make some woman a decent husband, but he was not for her. He was too prudish, too tame, too domesticated for her. As his wife she would have been safe, but she would never have been truly happy. Accepting him would have been a measure of her cowardice, not of her good sense.

He gave a short bark of laughter, but there was no mirth in it. "No, I would not."

"I didn't think so." It was strange how little the idea upset her. "I wouldn't marry me either, if I were in your position."

He steepled his fingers together and looked at her from over the top of them. "So, now we have agreed that any marriage between us is out of the question, what do you want from me?"

"I want to continue working here. As a nurse."

He raised his eyebrows. "Do you think that is wise? Or even desirable? I have to think about more than your continued employment—I have to think about the good name of the hospital."

"I'm a good nurse. You know I am."

"Your competence as a nurse is not in question. It is your fitness to act as a nurse that is in doubt."

She ignored his unspoken inference. "You could speak to the matron and get me reinstated if you chose to."

He did not deny it. "I think it would be best if you were to take some time away from the hospital. To work out what you really want in your life. And then in a few months, if you decide your calling is truly to become a nurse, and if you decide you are willing to make the personal sacrifices to continue working at St. Thomas's, then I will see if the matron will reconsider."

"I know I want to be a nurse. I know I want to stay here. Can you not speak to her now?"

He took up his pen and bent over his work again. "I will not speak to her until I am sure it is the right thing to do," he said as he scribbled. "As of now, I am far from convinced you are an appropriate person to have on the staff. Now, if there is nothing else I can do for you, I hope you will excuse me. I am behind on my work." And with that he waved her out.

Beatrice walked out of his office, down the corridor, and out on to the street.

She had been dismissed. She was unemployed. All her long years of training had come to this—being thrown out of her position because of a momentary lapse of her good sense and discretion.

The streets were busier than ever as she wandered back to

the boardinghouse. She wouldn't be able to call it home for much longer. Without any money coming in from her job as a nurse, she would have to vacate her room for another girl in a few weeks. Goodness knows where she would go.

Maybe it was time she had a long visit with one of her sisters. They were always so sensible and full of good advice, and could help her sort out the mess she had made of her life.

But not yet. Maybe in a week or so she would be able to face her family. Right now, her nerves felt too raw and her spirit too bruised. All she wanted was to crawl under her bedcovers and sleep for a week, and hope that everything had magically changed for the better by the time she woke up again.

Mrs. Bettina was in the kitchen with the cook kneading dough for bread when Beatrice arrived back. She wiped the flour off her hands with a damp cloth and hurried over to take Beatrice's arm. "It didn't go so well at the hospital, I take it?"

"I have been dismissed." She tried to choke back her tears, but faced with Mrs. Bettina's sympathy they insisted on falling. "I have nothing. No job. No man. I soon won't even have a place to live."

"You can stay here for as long as you please," Mrs. Bettina said loyally. "A good nurse like you will have twenty new offers of a position before too much longer. And you can pay me your back rent when you start working again."

Mrs. Bettina marched down to the hospital with all the determination of an avenging angel.

If anyone should be punished for Beatrice's unexpected absence from the hospital, it should be her.

The sergeant-major had told her what Captain Carterton was planning and she had done nothing to stop it. She'd thought that Captain Carterton was so much of a better match for Beatrice's spirit that she'd been willing to turn a blind eye to his shenanigans.

She marched straight into Matron Baddeley's office. A tiny room that had once been used as a storage closet, it was barely big enough for a tiny desk and a chair to sit at. Mrs. Bettina had to stand just inside the doorway to fit in at all.

The matron looked up, a false smile plastered on her face. "Mrs. Bettina, what an unexpected pleasure. What can I do for you?"

"I have come to see you about Miss Beatrice Clemens, one of your nurses."

The smile instantly faded from the matron's face. "I dismissed the girl this morning. She has already gone. There is nothing to worry about."

"That is exactly why I have come to see you. She has been boarding with me for several years and she is a fine girl. I cannot believe she deserves to be summarily dismissed."

"Miss Clemens has proven herself to be unreliable, and of poor character." The matron's voice scraped on her ear. "In my books, that is quite sufficient to warrant dismissal."

"She was not to blame for her absence. I have it on good authority that she did not go with the captain of her own free will."

"What a taradiddle." The matron's face was screwed up in an ugly laugh. "If you believe that, you will believe anything. The trollop has been caught out and now she thinks to escape the consequences of her debauchery by laying the blame elsewhere."

"Debauchery? Nonsense. She is a young woman with a woman's needs. What business is it of mine, or indeed of yours, if she chooses to spend her weekend in the company of a young man?"

The matron's face grew uglier still. "You are making excuses for her?"

"I am pointing out that whatever she does in her private life, she is a good nurse. Doesn't that count for anything? After all, which of us would not do the same as she if we had the chance?"

At her last, incautious words, the matron's eyes nearly popped out of her head in fury. "Are you accusing me of being as morally bankrupt as that young woman?"

Mrs. Bettina's own anger was growing. What an old hypocrite the matron was. Everyone in the hospital knew that each year she took in half a dozen likely young men as boarders, and each year chose one of them to live rent free in exchange for favors offered. "Are you telling me you wouldn't let some handsome young man climb into bed with you if he asked?"

The woman's face was incandescent with rage. "I have heard quite enough, thank you." Spittle flecked the corner of her mouth as she spoke. "You may leave my office now. In fact, you may leave the hospital. And do not come back."

"I have been employed as a private nurse here. I have a patient who needs me."

The matron gave a nasty cackle. "You should have thought of that before you called me nasty names. I will have no women like you or your Miss Clemens in my hospital. As of now, your position is terminated."

Mrs. Bettina stalked out of the matron's office, her hands shaking with anger. She had not made Beatrice's situation any better, and she had made her own worse. No one could hire a private nurse without the matron's say-so, and the matron was a petty tyrant who would neither forget nor forgive their quarrel.

She peeped in through the door to where the sergeant-major lay. His face brightened when he caught sight of her. "Nancy, my love, I'm right glad to see you. Aren't you a sight for sore eyes, then."

She lingered in the doorway, drinking in the sight of him. How she would miss him when she left. She doubted the matron would even let her in the door as a visitor now. "For sore legs, too, I hope," she said, trying to remain lighthearted, as she came over and sat beside him on the bed.

He took her hand in his and pressed it to his lips. "If anything could heal me faster, it would be you."

"I hope you will heal fast enough without me."

He looked at her questioningly. "What are you trying to tell me?"

She made an awkward face, halfway between a smile and a

grimace of apology. "I quarreled with the matron this morning. She requested in no uncertain terms that I remove myself from the hospital forthwith."

A cloud passed over his face. "Then you will not be coming back to see me?"

"I am sorry. I will miss your company." The words were so inadequate to express all she wanted to say.

"And I will miss yours. More than I can say."

They sat there in silence, hand in hand. Mrs. Bettina did not know what to say, how to say goodbye to the man in the bed who had come to mean so much to her in such a short space of time. Was it wrong to have fallen in love again at her age?

People would laugh at her if they knew how her heart beat in her aged chest at the sight of him. But did she not deserve love as much as any younger woman?

The sergeant-major cleared his throat. "I hate to have to ask you this, Nancy. I have no future and little to offer any woman and I hate to think that you might take me out of pity. But would you consider, would you possibly think about, becoming my wife?"

She froze. She hadn't expected him to offer her marriage. They had become lovers out of simple need. Each of them had needed what the other had given them. There had been no agreement between them, no understanding—just pure physical passion. She had not meant to fall in love with him, and had not expected him to return her foolish affections. "You are asking me to marry you?"

"I would get down on one knee and ask you, but I wouldn't be able to get up again."

Happiness was bubbling up inside her like water from a pure spring. "I don't know what to think, what to say." To think that he returned her love. To think that she had found a man to love her again after so long alone. She must be the most fortunate woman in all of England.

"You don't have to answer me now if you'd rather think on it." His voice was diffident, as if he expected her to laugh at him. "I'm only a sergeant-major, and this leg is going to see me invalided out of the army. I've got little enough in savings, and not even a house to take you to. If you take me, you'll only be getting a broken-down old soldier on half-pay. Not much of a bargain by anyone's standards. But I am fond of you, lass, and I'll do my best to be a good husband to you."

"I'm hardly much of a bargain myself." Honesty forced her into the admission. "I'm getting a bit long in the tooth. I'll never give you children."

"I can do without children. I never expected to be a father, and wouldn't miss it. But I can't do without you. I've been a bit of a rover in my youth. You are the only woman I've ever met who I could love with all my heart. The only one I have ever wanted to settle down with. I've seen enough of the world now. I could happily grow old in a cottage by the sea in your company."

"It doesn't matter that you'll be on half-pay. I have a comfortable boardinghouse that would give us enough income for us both to live on. You can save your pay for a pint of bitter at the local."

His face lit up then, as if a gaslight behind his eyes had been turned on. "Does that mean you'll have me?"

How could he ever have doubted it? He was offering her a chance at the kind of happiness she had thought was lost to her forever. "Of course I will. I would be honored to become your wife."

He pulled her down toward him and enfolded her in his arms. "How can I ever thank you enough? You are the best woman I have ever met, and I love you dearly."

She kissed him then, and ran her hand lightly over the graying stubble on his cheek. He was hers, all hers. She would take good care of him for the rest of her life. Never would he regret taking her as his wife. "I am the happiest woman in all of London, to have found a man as good as you are."

Lenora watched Dr. Hyde as he cast a perfunctory glance around the patients in the room. It was late and he should have gone home long ago, but he had stayed restlessly pacing the corridors of the hospital.

She knew what was bothering him. Beatrice Clemens and her captain, and the compromising position he had seen them in. Beatrice had found the man who heated her blood, and it wasn't Dr. Hyde.

Lenora couldn't be sorry. Dr. Hyde had never loved Beatrice. Not really. He had only ever seen one side of her—competent, composed Beatrice, the dedicated nurse. He had never known who she really was, or seen the streak of adventure that she kept hidden under her starched white uniform.

It had doubtless helped that Beatrice had beautiful wavy brown hair with golden highlights, a complexion like a rose, and a figure that made her plain white uniform look positively exotic. An enticement to sin.

She heaved a sigh as she thought about Beatrice's good looks. No one would ever call her an enticement to sin. Her hair was too red even to be called auburn, and her face had a tendency to go all red and blotchy whenever she felt shy or out of her depth. Which, around Dr. Hyde, was pretty much all the time.

It was a shame that he could not see beyond her lack of beauty to the person inside her. She would be good for him, she knew it. If only he could see her as a woman, not just as his devoted colleague.

Just then his pacing took him in her direction. He stopped short before colliding in to her. "Miss Coppins, what are you still doing here?"

To her annoyance, she could feel blotches of red disfigure her complexion as he addressed her. "Night duty, Dr. Hyde." He would think she was suffering from a terrible skin disease instead of from terminal embarrassment.

He stroked his goatee idly, his attention already having wandered off elsewhere. "Harrumph."

"Did you want me for anything?" she ventured, unwilling to leave him in such a state. She would feel the waves of frustration pouring off him, the overwhelming sense that he felt at sea.

"No, nothing."

She left the ward with a sigh and returned heavyhearted to the nurse's office at the end of the corridor. She could not help a man who did not want to help himself.

No sooner had she sat down at her desk to catch up on paperwork, then he was at the door. He leaned against the doorjamb, still stroking his beard. Her insides ached with love for him.

"Tell me, Miss Coppins, have I been wrong about women all along?"

She steepled her hands together and looked at him steadily. "What do you mean?"

"I was fond of Beatrice and thought she would make me a good wife. I thought she was fond of me in return. I was a gentleman, and treated her as a lady. As I would wish for my sister to be treated." He gave a laugh so harsh it would scour a bedpan clean. "But she didn't want to be treated as a lady. She chose a soldier over me. Even though he treated her like a common woman. Like a whore."

Lenora tried to keep her countenance, but her face was turning a more fiery red than usual. "He was treating her as a man treats the woman he loves." Beatrice had chosen her own path. It was not Dr. Hyde's part to criticize her choices.

"You know what he did to her. We saw them rutting like animals. And Beatrice was enjoying it. She was on her hands and knees with her rump in the air begging him to fuck her as if she were a common harlot." He took a handkerchief from his pocket and wiped the sweat off his forehead.

Her face turned redder and blotchier than ever at his language. "Would you rather she had hated it?"

"Beatrice is a gently bred young lady. Such creatures so not feel animal passions like men do."

Lenora shook her head. If only he knew what went on in her head at night he would not be so sure of himself and his silly notions about women not feeling desire. "What makes you think that?"

"Take you, for example. You would not have been moaning out your pleasure in the arms of a soldier and begging him to fuck you harder and faster."

"What makes you think that I am immune to passion? Because I am homely?" She gritted her teeth to hold in the frustration that threatened to explode out of her.

He looked at her as if he had never actually seen her before. "Homely? What nonsense. You are a lady."

"I am a woman." A woman who is deeply, desperately in love.

"You are no Beatrice."

"No, but I am still a woman."

"You would not behave in such a manner. And with such a man."

"My chastity has not yet been tested by a man I really want. If that were to happen, I do not know how I would respond." The thought of being in Dr. Hyde's arms, moaning with pleasure and begging him to fuck her harder and faster made her face hot enough to cook her dinner on. Lucky Beatrice, to have found a man to give her such wanton pleasure. Once again, she envied her friend. If ever she had the chance to behave in a similar fashion with Dr. Hyde, she knew exactly what she would do.

His eyes narrowed. "I do not believe you."

He was handing her the opportunity she needed on a plate. Did she have the courage to speak what she was feeling? Or would she live out the rest of her life with useless regrets?

She hesitated. No, she had enough regrets already. "Try me." Her voice was a mere breath of sound.

"If I were to ask you to bend over that desk and raise your skirts so I could fuck you," he said, fixing his eyes on hers and daring her to object to his deliberate crudity, "you would slap my face for insulting you. And I would deserve it."

"Try me."

"Ladies want to be treated with kid gloves, not taken roughly."

"Try me."

At her third invitation, his patience snapped. "Bend over the desk, then, Lenora." He crossed his arms and looked at her, confident in her refusal. "Bend over and beg me to fuck you like an animal just like Beatrice begged her soldier, if that's what you women really want."

Unhurriedly she rose to her feet, smoothing her hands down over her skirts to dry the nervous sweat. Whatever happened, she would not back down now. She did not *want* to back down, not with Dr. Hyde looking at her in such a predatory way, as if he were an eagle and she was a tasty mouse on which he was about to pounce.

She moved to the front of the desk and leaned over it until her bottom was raised high in the air in invitation. Then, with deliberate slowness, she started to lift her skirts.

Dr. Hyde swallowed to get rid of the dryness in his throat. Was that really Lenora in front of him, leaning over her desk and posturing in such a shameless fashion? As if she were a woman for sale? He ought to be repelled but instead he was desperately aroused.

He watched her, fascinated, picking up her skirts and lifting them, inch by torturous inch. First a pair of shapely ankles came into view, clad in buttoned-up black boots, then her calves. When her skirts were up to her thighs, showing the plump, bare flesh above the top of her stockings, he could stand it no longer. "Stop," he cried. "You do not want to be doing this."

"Yes, I do," was her calm response, and she kept on lifting until her skirts were around her waist.

She was wearing white bloomers, with lace around the edges. He ought to move away, prevent her somehow from behaving in such a wanton way, but he had to look.

Her hands crept under her skirts, and then her bloomers fell away, leaving her bottom exposed. Her rounded bottom, and that pink cleft between her thighs that called to him so strongly. "Fuck me, Dr. Hyde."

"You do not know what you are asking of me." He ought not be looking at a lady in such a lascivious way. He ought not be thinking of how good it would feel to plunge himself deep into her cunt, but he was. A force too strong for him to resist had him unbuttoning his trousers and taking out his cock. He was already stiffening, and a few strokes made him as hard as rock.

"Yes, I do." She gave her rump a little wiggle. Her cleft was moist and her lips looked swollen. Her entire body was begging him to touch her, to taste the forbidden paradise she was offering. "Come and take me. I know you want to. I bet your cock is hard as nails now, just looking at me."

He stepped closer to her, until she was trapped between his thighs, and placed his cock right at the opening of her cleft. The tip slid easily over her slickness, nudging apart her folds. "You are a lady. You should not want me to do this."

God help him, but he wanted it. He wanted to take her hard and rough, to fuck her until she cried out for more, just like Beatrice had called to her soldier. He was as capable of pleasing a woman as any soldier.

"But I do want it. Fuck me, Dr. Hyde."

He could have resisted a practiced seduction, but he was no match for the sweet pleading of an innocent. With a cry almost of pain, he gave in to his need and with one long, slow thrust, pushed inside her.

The mere act of entering her was almost enough to make him come. She felt like the softest bed, like the most delicious food, like the most heavenly scent all rolled into one. He wanted more of her. He could not stop himself from taking more.

Her bodice was fastened in the back with tiny pearl buttons. He did not wait to undo them, but wrenched them off. They pinged onto the floor and scattered in all directions.

Rough with need, he pushed her bodice down over her shoulders and took her breasts in both hands. Her nipples were tight and hard, and her breasts gloriously full. He'd never noticed before what delights lay under her starched white uniform, but now that he'd discovered them, he wanted to taste them all.

With his hands on her breasts, he slowly withdrew. Her muscles contracted around him, protesting his departure. But he had only withdrawn so he could thrust into her again, until his body was jammed against hers as close as it would go and he was buried in her soft body up to the hilt.

She moaned underneath him, but he could not tell whether it was from pain or pleasure.

Summoning the last vestiges of his self-control, he forced himself to stop moving. "Should I stop? Am I hurting you?" It would kill him to stop now, but he would do it if she asked him to.

"No, don't stop." She gave another moan, and pressed herself harder against him, encouraging him to go even deeper inside her. "You could never hurt me."

That was all the permission he needed to allow his desire to take over. With mindless abandon he poured himself into her.

She matched him, stroke for stroke, until he was afraid he

would spontaneously combust with the force of his desire. Just as he feared he could not hold out for a moment longer, he felt her muscles contract around him, and she cried out in ecstasy.

Her pleasure broke the last shreds of his self-control. With a guttural cry, he pushed into her once, twice more, and then he was lost to a world of sensation. His entire body was as stiff as his cock as his orgasm overtook him, overpowering him until he was helpless in its grip. Over and over the pleasure pulsed through his veins as his seed spurted into her with all the force of his years of abstinence behind it.

Lenora collapsed bonelessly onto the desk, her body racked with shudders.

Now that it was over, he felt a coil of shame grow inside him. Lenora was a fine woman. She deserved better than to be taken like a dog from behind. He reached out and stroked her hair. He loved her hair—it was the color of fire. And how she had burned him tonight. "I am sorry, Lenora. I did not mean to treat you so."

He should slide out of her and button himself up again, but he was loath to lose the moment of complete intimacy he shared with her. When had she crept into his heart like this? Or had he always known she was the woman for him? Was his courtship of Beatrice merely a trick to blind himself to the truth—that Lenora, gloriously plump, flame-haired Lenora, was the woman who took away his self-control and drove him to the point of madness?

"You are sorry for treating me as a man treats a woman?"

Lenora wriggled out from under him sounding more affronted than upset. "I can assure you, I need no apology. I enjoyed it quite as much as you did."

He adjusted his clothing then, too embarrassed at his dishevelment to look at her. "But—" What a foolish risk the pair of them had run. One of the patients could easily have wandered out into the corridor, peeked through the open office door and caught him with his trousers down, working away at her like a piston. What would that have done to her reputation?

"You can be sure that Beatrice's soldier did not apologize for taking her up to heaven."

He looked up into her bright blue eyes that held not a trace of guile. They were shining with satisfaction, and with something that looked suspiciously like love. "You mean, you did not mind?"

"Why should I mind? I have been dreaming of you making love to me for months."

How could he ever have believed that well-brought-up young women did not feel sexual desire? That it was wrong for them to do so? "I am glad of it, because I intend to repeat the experience with you as often as you will allow me to."

He had felt uncomfortable at the mere thought Beatrice might desire him, but he wanted Lenora to find him irresistible. Even though he had just taken her, already he was starting to harden at the thought that she might want him to fuck her again. Knowing that she loved the feeling of his cock inside her, the touch of his hands on her breasts, made him feel like a king.

She traced the contours of his bottom lip with the tip of her finger. "You know I could not refuse you anything."

He could not let this woman get away. "Then you will agree to be my wife? If I were to ask you with all my heart?"

"Your wife?" She gave a squeal of joy as she leaped into his arms. "Of course I will."

He enfolded her in his embrace. Nothing had ever felt as right as this did. In Lenora's arms, he had found where he belonged.

Thirteen

Captain Carterton sat in the kitchen of the deserted cottage nursing a snifter of the best French brandy. He had poured it out several hours ago and had still to finish drinking. It was a measure of how distraught he was over Beatrice that he couldn't summon up any interest in his favorite vice.

He shook his head as he forced another swallow. It burned all the way down his throat, numbing his stomach, but unfortunately leaving his brain intact. His mind was in turmoil, as it had been ever since he and Beatrice had been discovered together.

How could he have misread the situation so badly from the beginning? He'd thought her letters had come from the heart, but they had been nothing but an idle amusement. He'd thought he could win her heart, but it had been protected with walls of stone. He'd thought he could seduce her into his arms, and in that he had been right. But his success had only served in alienating her from him.

The worst of it was that he couldn't stop loving her. The thought that she had gone back to Dr. Hyde and begged him to overlook her folly in succumbing to another man had him feeling homicidal with rage. And with despair.

His fingers closed on the glass in his hand so hard that the snifter cracked, showering him with fragments of glass. He merely continued to sit there as the brandy soaked its way through his clothes.

Losing Beatrice was his own fault. He had pushed her too hard, and she had not been ready to accept all that he had to offer her. She was young, inexperienced. Until recently she had been a virgin. Was it any wonder she balked at being swept off her feet by a man she barely knew?

Beatrice was right to be cautious about him. Why would any girl, let alone a girl as beautiful as Beatrice, marry an officer who had only just escaped one war with his life intact, and who might be posted off to any other battleground in the Empire at any moment? He had an uncertain profession, and they lived in uncertain times. That was his only excuse for being so hasty in his courtship, and pushing his haste on her until she could not bear it.

He had promised Beatrice that he would not come running after her, but would leave her to make her own decision. It was the least he could do, after shamelessly pressuring her into falling in with his wishes, his plans. Whatever happened now would be up to fate, not to him.

But it never hurt to give fate a helping hand. Beatrice

needed to know that he still loved her, that he was sorry for his actions.

And what better way to explain himself than in one last letter.

Beatrice sat in her room, silently brooding. She hated being un-employed. This morning she had gathered her courage in both hands and applied for a position at another hospital, a lesser one than St. Thomas's. She'd given the matron her name, and a frosty look had come into the woman's eyes. The interview had been cut short soon afterward.

She would not be given a post there—she knew it. Matron Baddeley must have seen to it that her fall from grace was known throughout all the hospitals in London out of sheer spite.

She hated being unemployed. She hated Matron Baddeley who had dismissed her. She hated Dr. Hyde who had refused to reemploy her and who was now, to everyone's surprise, en-gaged to Lenora Coppins and looking quite ecstatic about it. Most of all she hated Captain Carterton who had brought all this misery on her.

No, she didn't hate Captain Carterton. That was part of the problem. She was horribly afraid that she was in love with him.

She could tell herself over and over again that it was her po-sition as a nurse she missed most in her current situation, but she would be lying. What she wanted most of all was to feel the captain's hands on her, and the sounds of his voice telling her that he loved her.

How could she have been so blind to his small kindnesses, to the little generosities that marked him out as a kind, good-hearted man? She had been afraid of him, of what he could do to her, of the mess he was making in her orderly world. And her fear had caused her to break the heart of a man who truly cared for her.

His last words to her had not been a dismissal, but a goodbye. He was sick of feeling unloved, of being rejected. Didn't that mean he still loved her? That he would welcome her back?

Quickly, before she lost her courage, she picked up a sheet of paper.

Back at the barracks, Captain Carterton sat moodily over his breakfast eggs and kippers. He had to be prepared for the worst, for Beatrice to soundly reject him. Or worse, to leave him with no answer at all, with the agony of hope but no resolution.

He would give her a week, maybe two. If he had not heard by then, he would squelch his hope into the furthermost corner of his soul and forget about it there.

The officers' batman passed by him, a silver salver on his hand. "The morning post, sir."

Carterton laid down his fork and picked up the letter with a decided lack of interest.

When he saw the handwriting, his heart stopped beating. With deliberate movements, he picked up the letter opener from the silver tray, slit the seal, and handed the letter opener to the batman. "Thank you, Willis."

With shaking hands, he began to read.

Temptation

Dear Percy,

I find myself in the rather awkward position of admitting to myself that two courses of action I have recently taken have caused my life to start down a path that I do not wish to travel. I'm hoping you will be able to assist me in navigating back to a more favorable route.

Love is a fickle thing, sometimes it pulls one in an unexpected direction. Perhaps it is like the blinkered view of the horse at the harness, myopic and sadly ignorant of things going on outside of the periphery. And then, like iron pyrites masquerading as gold, sometimes love can be fake, misleading. The golden glow, true or false, causes people to change, to do uncharacteristic things. I am guilty in this regard . . .

Beatrice was in the kitchen with Mrs. Bettina making pastry for a peach pie when the doorbell rang. Since being dismissed from her post at St. Thomas's Hospital, she had filled in her days helping out around the boardinghouse in return for cheaper rent. There was always so much to do, cooking, cleaning, laundry. Mrs. Bettina had gone up several notches in her estimation in the last weeks—she worked so hard every day looking after her houseful of lodgers.

She dusted the flour off her hands, gave them a quick wipe on her apron, and went to answer the door.

The post boy handed her a letter, tipped his cap to her, and was gone.

She stood there in the door, motionless, staring at the letter in her hand.

She had only sent her letter to him this morning. It was too early for him even to have received it, let alone have written her a reply. Had she been too late? Was this his final farewell?

Her legs could not hold her for another moment. She sat down on the stoop and ripped the letter open with trembling fingers.

Dear Beatrice,

I'm writing in the hope that you have not immediately thrown this letter's unopened envelope into the privy, and that you have at least gotten this far by unfolding these pages and reading this paragraph. Dearest Beatrice, I implore you to read on to the end, at which point you have, of course, the choice to reply. Or not.

I must start by telling you I must be the most foolish man on this earth. Truly, I do not know what possessed me to have treated you so. Jealousy, stupidity, desire, all of these things are reasons but not excuses. These emotions, these pains, they flow through me whenever I think of you. Is this love? I think it must be . . .

Captain Carterton put on his smartest dress uniform, and pomaded his hair with care. He did not want to give Beatrice a single reason to look on him with disfavor. Out of the kindness of her heart she had given him another chance, and this time he would not squander it.

Her letter was lying open on his dressing table. Though he knew every line of it by heart, his eyes were drawn to her precious words.

Temptation

. . . Have you ever watched waves crash onto a cliff face? The wave will hit the wall with a shower of spray, then reflect back out to sea where it encounters other incoming waves. Sometimes the waves will interact negatively, canceling each other out. But sometimes they intersect and become as one, only twice as powerful. I fear Dr. Hyde and myself were like the former, when we are together we become nothing. But I was afraid of what you and I, together, would be . . .

Beatrice closed her eyes and leaned her head against the doorframe. Thank heavens it was not too late. She still had a chance with the captain. She clutched the letter tightly in her hand as she made her way up to her room to read it through again. The pastry crust would spoil, but no matter. She would turn it into a peach cobbler and no one would notice.

Safely up in her room, she spread the pages over her bed.

. . . I am sitting at my desk a penitent man. I made mistakes, I'm guilty of the sins of lust, envy, pride, anger. Like Dante I need a Beatrice to guide me to heaven. I am hoping, praying, that you will be my Beatrice, my savior.

She sighed. How gladly she would take that role. If he gave her another chance, she would take him to heaven every day of his life.

> *. . . I do not write this to pressure you, my love. I know that your love cannot be commanded, and I have already shamed myself far, far too much trying to command yours.*
>
> *I will wait for your forgiveness until I no longer have any hope at all.*
>
> *If ever you want me, I am yours.*
>
> Percy

She hugged the pages to her chest. She had forgiven him long ago. All he had done was done for love of her.

The streets were so full of horse and foot traffic Captain Carterton decided walking would be quicker than hailing a hansom cab.

He set out at a brisk pace, Beatrice's letter tucked safely in his breast pocket and her last words running through his head.

> *. . . In my treatment of you I have proven myself to be a coward, valuing security over affection. I am not proud of that. Even now, it is taking more courage than I possess to reach out to you. I am being brave for your sake, because I do not want to lose you.*
>
> *I am not brave enough to marry you until I know you better—I cannot take such a step yet. But I promise you I will let you into my heart. I promise you I will give our passion a chance to develop into a lasting love.*
>
> *If you still want me, I am yours.*
>
> Beatrice

If he still wanted her? He shook his head as he strode along. He would want her until the day he died. There was no woman on earth for him but Beatrice.

The door to the boardinghouse was slightly ajar. He rapped on it with the head of his cane. If she was not at home, he would sit and wait for her, all day if necessary. They had already wasted too much time apart.

There was a sound of feet positively running down the stairs and the door flew open. Beatrice, her hair loose around her shoulders and her dress covered in a floury apron, stood there in front of him, a smile of hope and fear on her face.

He held out his arms to her just as he had on the first night. "Beatrice, my love."

She ran into them, wrapping her own arms around him as if she would never let him go. "Thank heavens we are together at last."

Epilogue

Sergeant-Major Bartholomew Tofts, V.C. (Ret'd) stood on the front steps, awaiting the arrival of the carriage for the Carter-tons. The lucky young captain—he still couldn't think of him as Percy—had been married to the delightful Beatrice Clemens for nigh on a year now. And over that year he'd watched the couple grow together day by day.

He waited patiently, ramrod straight despite his years and injury, gripping his cane that was now his constant compan-ion a little more tightly as a spasm of pain shot up his leg. He cursed under his breath, reminding himself for the hundredth time not to put so much weight on that leg. It had never quite recovered after the stint in South Africa that had invalided him out of the army. Not that he ever regretted his injury, for if his leg had not been shot to pieces, he would never have met his wife. His Nancy would be worth the loss of both his legs.

Behind, the door opened and the Captain and Mrs. Carterton

joined him on the steps. He turned to greet the couple's arrival with a slight feeling of sadness. This was to be their last good-bye, and he'd grown to think of the captain quite as a son, the son he'd never had. "You look after the captain, now, Mrs. Carterton." He had to stop to clear his throat. "You know he's dear to me after all we've been through together."

Mrs. Carterton gave him a beatific smile. "I'll look after him, sir. And you must promise to be good to Mrs. Tofts for me. I want to return to these steps in a year or two and have her greet me, hale and hearty as ever."

"Aye, me and Mrs. Tofts, we're closer than two peas in a pod. I'll look after her all right. She's one in a million, and I'm lucky to have her. And are you excited to be going at last?"

Mrs. Carterton blinked. "I'm a mite nervous," she confessed in a whisper. "I've never been any further than Bristol, and now here I am leaving lovely green England for dusty, sandy Egypt to be a nurse in a makeshift hospital dealing with patients who suffer from all sorts of strange tropical illnesses. Nothing will be familiar."

"I'll be familiar," the captain offered with his ever-ready grin. "I promise you I'll be as familiar as I can be."

"Oh, Percy! You are incorrigible. Just you wait until it's time for your next vaccination. Then you'll see how familiar *I* can be."

Bartholomew looked on, both embarrassed and a little proud to see the youngsters tease each other with such fondness.

"I know we're leaving our little estate in good hands," the

captain said. "Do whatever you think best to keep things running smoothly."

He gave a smart salute to acknowledge the order. "Not to worry, captain, the animals will be bigger and fatter when you return, the grounds well looked after. And you ride those lads hard over in the Suez—don't let them get slack. The new company sergeant-major is just a whipper-snapper—he'll be needing a firm hand to keep things in line."

Their small talk faded to an awkward silence as the carriage, laden with their effects, rattled up to the door.

Sergeant-Major Tofts, recipient of his country's highest medal for valor, cleared his throat of a lump that had mysteriously appeared. "Well, this is it, then. Off you go. Travel safe."

He was surprised when Beatrice gave him a hug and a kiss on the cheek. "Thank you, sergeant-major. Keep well."

He had to blink furiously to clear his vision as he offered her a steady hand to climb into the carriage.

Turning to face Captain Carterton, he shook the young man's hand but could say no more. Unexpectedly Percy gave him a hug, as a son would a father.

Though he cleared his throat several more times, a hoarse "farewell" was all he could muster.

Percy clambered into the carriage to sit beside his wife, and barely had the door closed when the carriage jerked into motion, the horses clearly eager to get going. The carriage clattered down the drive and the sergeant-major waved goodbye. Neither of the couple saw him, but he didn't mind.

Temptation

Silhouetted in the back window he could see Beatrice's head resting on Percy's shoulder. Just before the carriage turned the corner out of sight, Percy turned to his wife and kissed her with all the ardor of a man in love.

A smile on his face, he turned to go back into the house, back to where his Nancy was waiting for him.

Those two would deal together well enough. They loved each other, and that was what mattered the most.

LEDA SWANN is the writing duet of Cathy and Brent. They write out of their home overlooking the sea in peaceful New Zealand. When not writing they have busy lives working in the technology industry, bringing up four children, and enjoying an adventurous outdoor life that ranges from the mountains to the sea.

Leda Swann